和孩子一起读诗

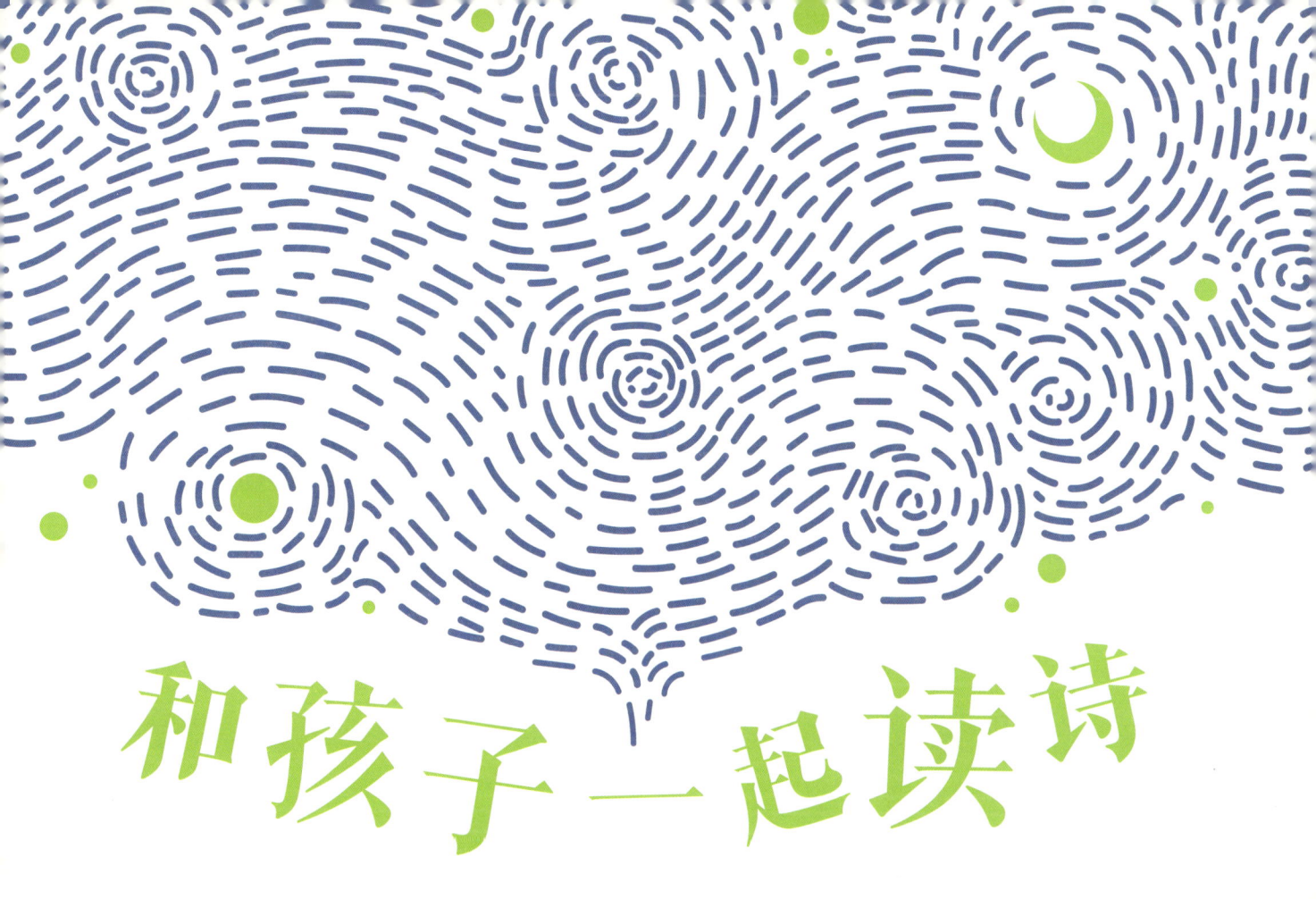

大师写给孩子的80首经典诗歌

[英] 约翰·济慈
[爱尔兰] 威廉·巴特勒·叶芝 等著

马永波 译

中国国际广播出版社

图书在版编目（CIP）数据

和孩子一起读诗 /（英）约翰·济慈等著；马永波译. —北京：中国国际广播出版社，2023.11
ISBN 978-7-5078-5434-3

Ⅰ.①和… Ⅱ.①约…②马… Ⅲ.①诗集－世界－现代 Ⅳ.①I12

中国国家版本馆CIP数据核字（2023）第214482号

和孩子一起读诗

著　　者	［英］约翰·济慈 等
译　　者	马永波
责任编辑	梁　媛
校　　对	张　娜
封面设计	王广福　黄紫涵
版式设计	邢秀娟

出版发行	中国国际广播出版社有限公司［010-89508207（传真）］
社　　址	北京市丰台区榴乡路88号石榴中心2号楼1701
	邮编：100079
印　　刷	北京启航东方印刷有限公司

开　　本	889×1194　1/16
字　　数	170千字
印　　张	13.5
版　　次	2023年12月 北京第一版
印　　次	2023年12月 第一次印刷
定　　价	68.00元

版权所有　盗版必究

目录 CONTENTS

001 第一辑 童年

003 一年的十二个月份 —— • 萨拉·柯勒律治

005 兄妹俩 —— • 列维斯·卡洛尔

006 男孩之歌 —— • 詹姆斯·霍格

008 独自 —— • 埃德加·爱伦·坡

010 有个老头胡子长 —— • 爱德华·利尔

012 奥西曼迪斯 —— • 珀西·比希·雪莱

014 明妮和温妮 —— • 阿尔弗雷德·丁尼生

016 老太婆麦格 —— • 约翰·济慈

018 给我的兄弟 —— • 约翰·济慈

020 所有的钟都在鸣响 —— • 克里斯蒂娜·吉奥尔吉娜·罗塞蒂

022 如果小猪戴假发 —— • 克里斯蒂娜·吉奥尔吉娜·罗塞蒂

024 谁曾见过风？ —— • 克里斯蒂娜·吉奥尔吉娜·罗塞蒂

026 微小的事物 —— • 茱莉亚·阿比盖尔·弗莱彻·卡妮

028 夜 —— • 威廉·布莱克

030 一个梦 —— • 威廉·布莱克

032 梦境 —— • 塞西尔·弗朗西斯·亚历山大

034 我的影子 —— • 罗伯特·路易斯·斯蒂文森

036 每当我看见天上的彩虹 —— • 威廉·华兹华斯

038 一个赤脚奔跑的婴儿 —— • 戴维·赫伯特·劳伦斯

041　第二辑　生灵

042　蝈蝈和蟋蟀 ──• 约翰·济慈

044　母牛 ──• 罗伯特·路易斯·斯蒂文森

046　苍蝇 ──• 威廉·布莱克

048　小羊羔 ──• 威廉·布莱克

050　老虎 ──• 威廉·布莱克

052　田鼠 ──• 塞西尔·弗朗西斯·亚历山大

054　致蝴蝶 ──• 威廉·华兹华斯

056　鹰 ──• 阿尔弗雷德·丁尼生

058　猫头鹰 ──• 阿尔弗雷德·丁尼生

060　蜂鸟 ──• 戴维·赫伯特·劳伦斯

062　鸭子的小调 ──• 肯尼斯·格雷厄姆

064　两只小猫 ──• 珍·泰勒

066　蜘蛛 ──• 珍·泰勒

068　一只小鸟沿小径走来 ──• 艾米莉·狄金森

070　草丛中一个细长的家伙 ──• 艾米莉·狄金森

072　猫和月亮 ──• 威廉·巴特勒·叶芝

074　小蜜蜂何其忙碌 ──• 艾萨克·瓦茨

077　鹰的嬉戏 ──• 沃尔特·惠特曼

078　一只沉默而坚忍的蜘蛛 ──• 沃尔特·惠特曼

081　第三辑　世界

083　希望是带羽毛的东西 ──• 艾米莉·狄金森

084　我是无名之辈！你是谁？ ──• 艾米莉·狄金森

085　没有一艘快船能像一本书 ── ● 艾米莉·狄金森

086　雪 ── ● 菲利普·爱德华·托马斯

088　回答一个孩子的问题 ── ● 塞缪尔·泰勒·柯勒律治

090　致水仙 ── ● 罗伯特·赫里克

092　秋天的火焰 ── ● 罗伯特·路易斯·斯蒂文森

094　大风夜 ── ● 罗伯特·路易斯·斯蒂文森

095　燧石 ── ● 克里斯蒂娜·吉奥尔吉娜·罗塞蒂

096　顿悟 ── ● 但丁·加百利·罗塞蒂

098　我 ── ● 沃尔特·德·拉·梅尔

100　诗人的歌 ── ● 阿尔弗雷德·丁尼生

102　万物明亮又美丽 ── ● 塞西尔·弗朗西斯·亚历山大

104　咒语 ── ● 艾米莉·勃朗特

106　黄金国度 ── ● 埃德加·爱伦·坡

108　人的四季 ── ● 约翰·济慈

110　花园围墙那边 ── ● 依里诺尔·法吉恩

112　那是在很久以前 ── ● 依里诺尔·法吉恩

114　打哈欠 ── ● 依里诺尔·法吉恩

116　在下午的山岗上 ── ● 埃德娜·圣·文森特·米莱

118　未来 ── ● 夏尔·克罗

121　第四辑　自然及其他

122　秋颂 ── ● 约翰·济慈

124　多少诗人给时间的流逝镀上了金 ── ● 约翰·济慈

126　啊,孤独!如果我必须与你同住 ── ● 约翰·济慈

128　黄水仙 ── ● 威廉·华兹华斯

130　啊，向日葵 ── •威廉·布莱克

132　一片残雪 ── •罗伯特·弗罗斯特

134　未走的路 ── •罗伯特·弗罗斯特

136　雪夜林边驻足 ── •罗伯特·弗罗斯特

138　茵尼斯弗利湖岛 ── •威廉·巴特勒·叶芝

140　美德 ── •乔治·赫伯特

142　本能 ── •伊迪特·伊蕾内·索德格朗

144　我童年的树木 ── •伊迪特·伊蕾内·索德格朗

146　林中湖泊 ── •伊迪特·伊蕾内·索德格朗

148　星 ── •伊迪特·伊蕾内·索德格朗

150　我看见路易斯安那有一棵橡树在生长 ── •沃尔特·惠特曼

152　当我听到那博学的天文学家 ── •沃尔特·惠特曼

154　奇迹 ── •沃尔特·惠特曼

156　记忆 ── •托马斯·贝利·奥尔德里奇

158　致水鸟 ── •威廉·卡伦·布莱恩特

160　缪斯 ── •安娜·安德烈耶夫娜·阿赫玛托娃

162　我不与人争 ── •沃尔特·萨维奇·兰多

163　《和孩子一起读诗》英文篇
203　作者介绍
209　后　记

第一辑 童年

费利克斯·布拉尔 绘

温斯洛·霍默 绘

一年的十二个月份

萨拉·柯勒律治

一月带来白雪，
脚趾手指都闪耀着光泽。

二月带来雨水，
冰封的池塘再次解冻。

三月带来微风尖锐响亮，
吹得水仙花翩翩起舞。

四月带来甜蜜的报春花，
在我们的脚旁把雏菊播撒。

五月带来一群群可爱的羊羔，
在毛发松软的母亲身边蹦蹦跳跳。

六月带来郁金香，百合与玫瑰，
让孩子们的手里花束满满。

炎热的七月带来凉爽的阵雨，
草莓和康乃馨。

八月带来成捆的稻谷，
丰收成果盈满了仓廪。

温暖的九月带来了果实，
猎人的枪声一阵阵响起。

清新的十月带来了山鸡，
采集坚果多让人欢喜。

沉闷的十一月带来了枯萎，
树叶很快就会纷纷飘坠。

寒冷的十二月带来了雨夹雪，
闪耀的炉火和圣诞欢歌。

杰西·威尔科克斯·史密斯 绘

兄妹俩

列维斯·卡洛尔

"小妹,小妹,快点上床!
去歇歇你疲倦的小脑袋。"
谨慎的哥哥这样说。

"你是想被揍得到处躲,
还是想脸上被挠开花?"
沉静的妹妹这样答。

"小妹,不要惹火我。
把你炖成一锅肉汤,
就像捻死个飞蛾!"

妹妹眯缝起眼睛,
抬头怒视着哥哥,
厉声道:"那就来试试!"

哥哥迅速奔进厨房。
"亲爱的厨娘,请借我一口锅,
越快越好。"

"我为什么要借给你锅呢?"
"厨娘,理由嘛,显而易见。
我想做一锅爱尔兰炖肉。"

"你要炖什么肉啊?"
"我妹妹将为锅中之物!"
"哇哦!"
"你会借给我锅吗,厨娘?"
"不会!"

格言云:别把你妹妹给炖了。

男孩之歌

詹姆斯·霍格

那里的池塘又亮又深，
那里有灰鳟鱼在沉睡，
沿河而上，越过牧场，
那条路只属于我和比利。

那里的黑鸟唱到最晚，
那里的山楂花开得最甜，
那里的雏鸟叽喳又飞窜，
那条路只属于我和比利。

那里的人割草最干净，
那里的干草堆又厚又绿；
追随归巢的蜜蜂，
那条路只属于我和比利。

那里的榛树岸最为陡峭，
那里的阴影降落在深谷，
那里有成串的坚果随意掉落，
那条路只属于我和比利。

为什么男孩子们的游戏
要赶走甜美的小女生，
为什么他们更喜欢玩笑和打仗，
那件事我始终弄不懂。

可我知道，我喜欢游荡，
穿过草场，在干草垛之间；
沿河而上，越过牧场，
那条路只属于我和比利。

杰西·威尔科克斯·史密斯 绘

独自

埃德加·爱伦·坡

从童年起我就与众不同,
我不像其他人那样看待事物,
我无法从普通的源泉中
汲取自己的激情。
我的悲哀并非有同样的起源,
同样的声调也无法唤起我心中的欢乐;
我所爱的一切,我都是独自爱着。
那时,在我的童年时代,
在最为动荡的生命的黎明
从善与恶的深渊中
我汲取了那依然将我紧缚的奥秘:

从激流,从泉水,
从大山红色的峭壁,
从围绕我旋转的
发散秋日金黄的太阳,
从天空中的闪电,
当它从我身旁一掠而过,
从雷声与风暴,
还有,当天空一派湛蓝
在我的瞭望中
显现出的魔鬼般的云彩。

杰西·威尔科克斯·史密斯 绘

有个老头胡子长

爱德华·利尔

有个老头胡子长,
他说:"我就怕这样!——
两只猫头鹰,一只母鸡,
四只云雀和一只鹪鹩
全都把巢筑在我的胡子上!"

弗雷德里克·摩根 绘

奥西曼迪斯

珀西·比希·雪莱

一个古国的游客曾对我言称:
有两条巨大的石腿立于沙漠
失落了躯干……附近沙地之中,
半掩半埋,一只残破的人头仰卧,
蹙额皱眉,犹自撮唇施令,
雕刻者深谙此般傲慢冷酷的激情
将其烙印于了无生机的石头上,
那仿效的手和独运的匠心已消失无踪;
像座上隐隐现出如许字样:
"吾乃奥西曼迪斯,万王之王,
丰功伟业,令强者绝望!"
此外无一物幸存。残骸周围
唯余莽莽平沙,无边无垠
光秃寂寥,伸向远方。

马科斯菲尔德·帕里斯 绘

明妮和温妮

阿尔弗雷德·丁尼生

明妮和温妮
睡在贝壳里。
睡吧,乖小姐!
甜甜地睡吧。

贝壳里面粉莹莹,
外面一片银光;
大海的声音
在周围游荡。

睡吧,乖小姐,
不要那么早醒来!

回声重重叠叠,
消逝在月亮那边。

两颗闪闪的亮星
向贝壳里面窥望。
"谁能告诉我们,
她们梦中的光景?"

一只绿色的朱顶雀
从谷仓中惊飞;
醒醒,乖小姐,
太阳漂在了海上!

杰西·威尔科克斯·史密斯 绘

老太婆麦格

约翰·济慈

老麦格是个吉卜赛，
她一个人住在野外；
她的床是棕色的石南草皮，
她的家就是无遮无盖。

她的苹果是有毒的黑莓，
她的红醋栗长在扫帚上；
她的酒是白色野玫瑰的露，
她的书是一座坟墓。

她的兄弟们是陡峭的峰峦，
她的姐妹们是落叶的松树——
与这个大家庭同在，
她过得心满意足。

很多时候她没有早餐，
很多时候她也没有午餐，
代替了晚餐，她盯着月亮
苦苦地睁大了双眼。

可在每一个忍冬花初绽的黎明
她都把鲜艳的花环制作，
每一个幽谷紫杉暗淡的夜晚
她都会编织，并且歌唱。

她用衰老发黄的手指，
把灯芯草垫编织
分发给丛林里
遇见的村民。

老麦格和玛丽皇后一样勇敢，
像亚马逊人一样高大；
她穿着红色的旧袍子；
头戴一顶破草帽。
上帝让她的老骨头终于休息——
很久以前她已不在人世。

温斯洛·霍默 绘

给我的兄弟

约翰·济慈

小火苗在新添的煤块间欢闹,
微弱的噼啪声轻轻爬过岑寂
如同家神在暗中轻声细语
为兄弟之情保守一个温柔的帝国。
这时啊,我精骛八极,求索诗韵,
你们的眼睛,宛若在诗的梦里,
紧盯着那滔滔不绝的深奥传说,
当夜幕降临,安慰着我们的愁烦。
今天是你的生日,汤姆,我欣喜
这一天过得顺利,过得安详。
愿我们还能共度许多这样的静夜
温柔地低语,沉静地享受这世间
真正的快乐,在那伟大的声音
和蔼地盼咐我们的灵魂飞升之前。

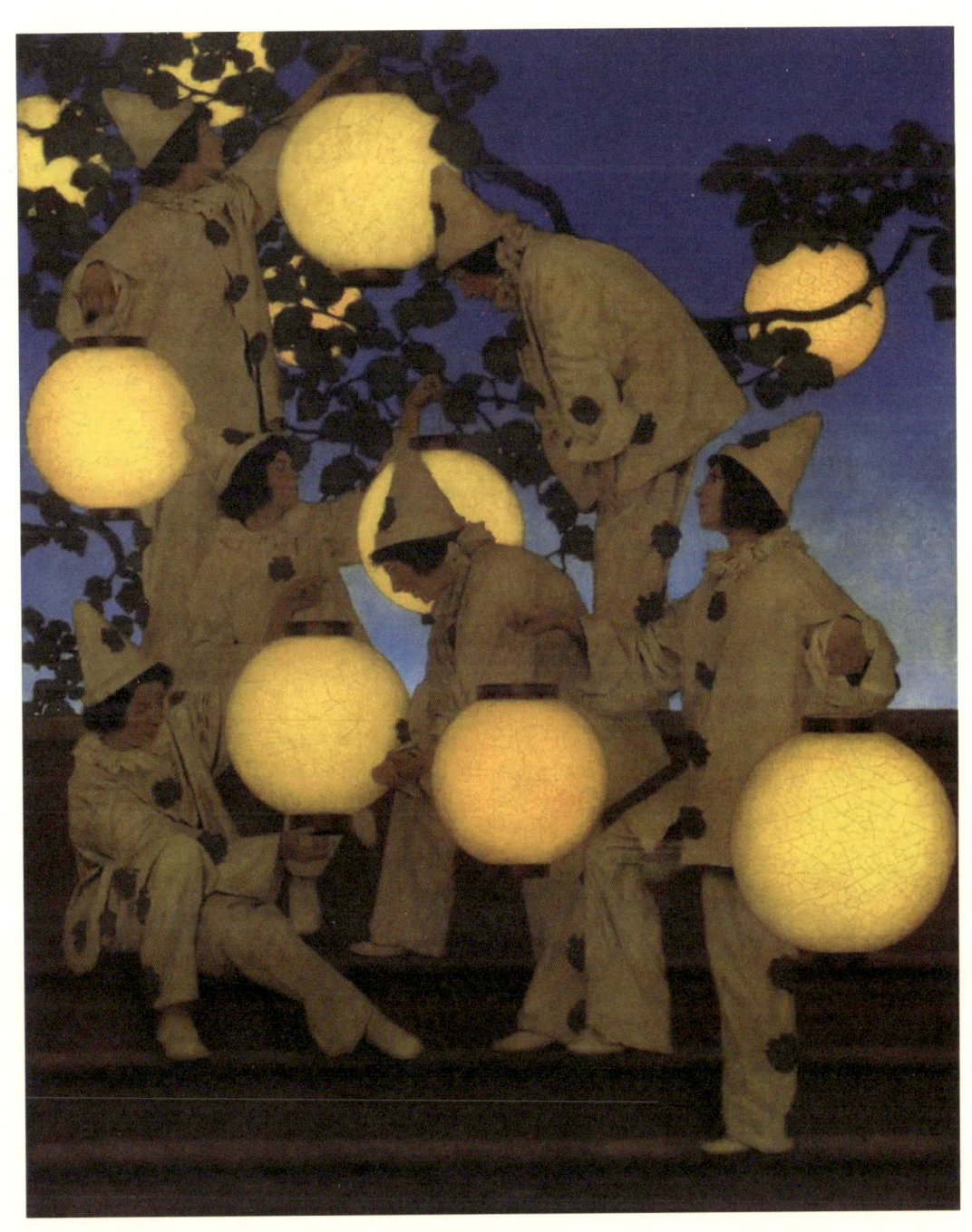

马科斯菲尔德·帕里斯 绘

所有的钟都在鸣响

克里斯蒂娜·吉奥尔吉娜·罗塞蒂

所有的钟都在鸣响,
所有的鸟儿都在歌唱,
当莫莉坐下来哭泣,
哭她破碎的洋娃娃;
哦,你这傻莫莉!
抽咽着,叹息着,
哭一只破碎的洋娃娃,
当所有的钟都在鸣响,
当所有的鸟儿都在歌唱。

杰西·威尔科克斯·史密斯 绘

如果小猪戴假发

克里斯蒂娜·吉奥尔吉娜·罗塞蒂

如果小猪戴假发,
我们该怎么说?
把他当作绅士,
和他说:"天气真不错。"

如果他的尾巴掉了,
我们该怎么做?
送他去女裁缝那里
给他换条新的。

威廉·亨利·德特勒夫·科纳 绘

谁曾见过风?

克里斯蒂娜·吉奥尔吉娜·罗塞蒂

谁曾见过风?
不是我,也不是你;
可当树叶颤抖,
是风在从中穿过。

谁曾见过风?
不是你,也不是我;
可当大树低下头,
是风在从旁经过。

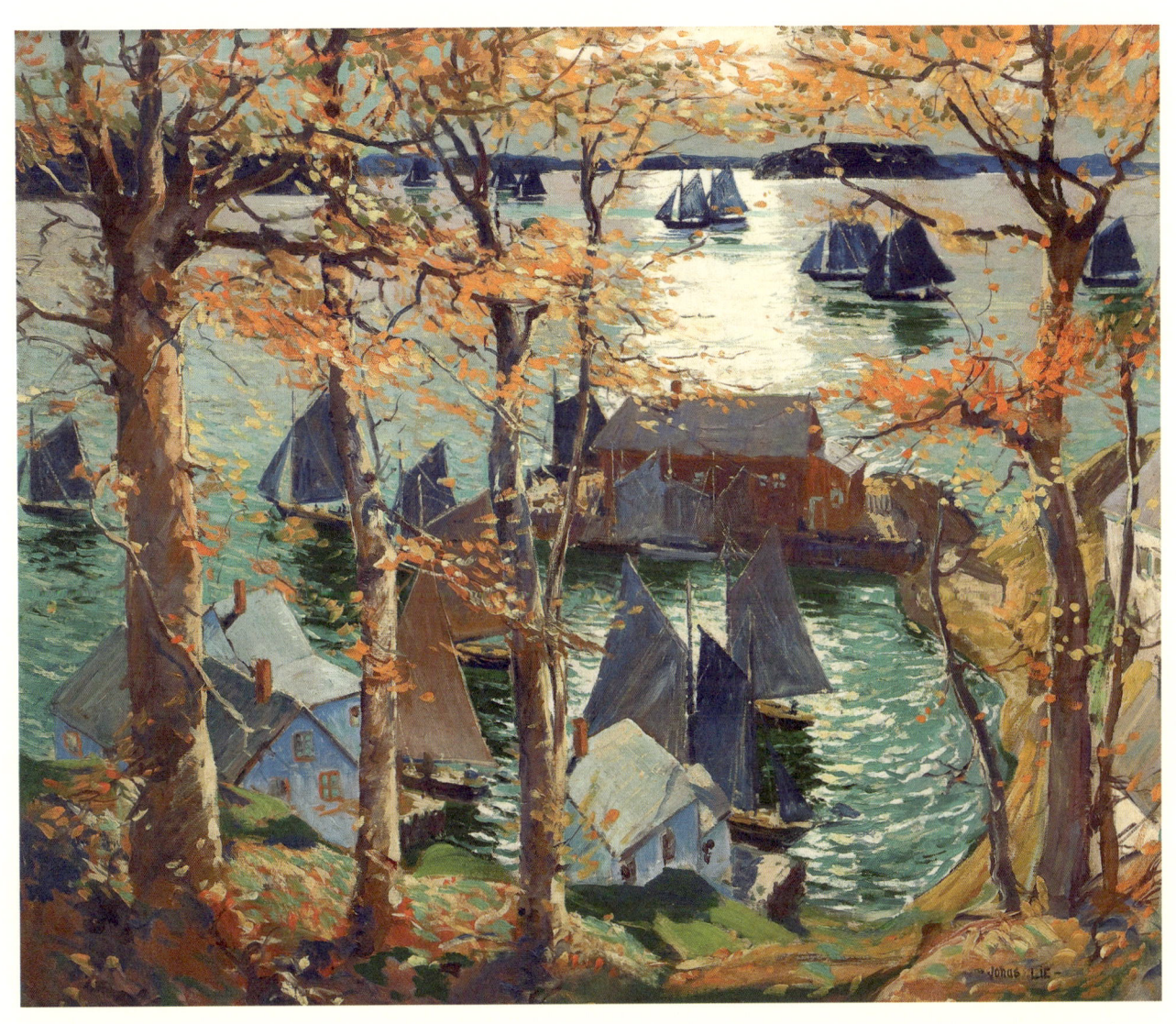

乔纳斯·李 绘

微小的事物

茱莉亚·阿比盖尔·弗莱彻·卡妮

小小的雨点，
小小的沙粒，
构成浩瀚的海洋
美妙的大地。

短暂的瞬间，
尽管卑微，
却构成了永恒
漫长的年岁。

我们小小的错误
使灵魂偏离，
美德的路途
在罪中迷失。

小小的善举，
小小的爱的语言，
使我们的地球，
成为人间乐园。

杰西·威尔科克斯·史密斯 绘

夜

威廉·布莱克

太阳在西天沉落,
晚星光芒闪耀;
鸟儿在巢中静息,
我也要寻找自己的巢。
月亮像一朵花儿,
高高地在天庭悬挂,
怀着静静的喜悦,
对着夜晚微笑。

再见,绿野和幸福的小树林,
在那里羊群多么欢欣;
在那里羊羔啃着青草,
天使的脚步轻轻移动;
他们无形地将欢乐和祝福,
永无止息地倾注,
在每一朵蓓蕾和鲜花上,
在每一颗安睡的心上。

他们探望疏忽的鸟巢,
把鸟儿暖暖地遮盖;
他们探访野兽的洞穴,
不让它们受到伤害。
如果他们看见有谁
哭泣着不肯安睡,
就会把睡意洒在它们头上,
然后坐在它们身旁。

当虎狼嚎叫着捕猎,
他们就站住,悲悯地哭泣;
试图驱散它们的饥渴,
把它们和羊群隔离。
但它们若可怕地向前冲去,
天使们就小心翼翼,
接受每一个温柔的灵魂,
安居在新的世界。

那里狮子红色的眼睛
将会流出金色的泪水,
并怜悯那些温柔的呼声,
在羊栏周围徘徊,
说道:"他以柔顺将暴怒,
以健康将疾病
驱逐出了
我们永恒的时日。"

"咩咩叫的羔羊,在你身边,
我现在可以躺下睡去;
或想着以你为名的他,
跟在你后面吃草,哭泣。
因为我在生命之河,
洗过了闪亮的鬃毛,
它将永远金光闪闪,
当我守护着羊栏。"

杰西·威尔科克斯·史密斯 绘

一个梦

威廉·布莱克

曾有一个梦编织了一片浓荫
在我那天使守护的床顶,
我以为自己是躺在青草上
见一只蚂蚁迷失了方向。

苦恼,茫然,凄惨而绝望,
夜色黑了,她疲惫又彷徨,
越过许多纠结的草叶,
心碎神伤,我听见她说:

"我的孩子们啊!他们在哭泣,
他们可曾听到父亲的叹息?

他们一会儿四处去把我寻找,
一会儿又回去,为我哭号。"

我落下一滴眼泪,出于同情,
但是我看见来了一只萤火虫,
他应道:"是谁在哭泣悲哀,
把我这夜的守望者唤来?"

"我就要照亮这片大地,
还有甲虫到处巡视;
现在,跟随甲虫的嗡鸣,
小小流浪者,快快回家!"

杰西·威尔科克斯·史密斯 绘

梦境

塞西尔·弗朗西斯·亚历山大

遥远，遥远的山巅那边，
越过灰色的石头和山岩，
越过暗绿色绵延的松林，
它覆盖着大山西侧的山肩，
就是我那神话的国土，
没有任何人曾把它看见。

它的水果像是罕见的红宝石，
它的溪流像玻璃一般清澈，
那里有金色的城堡高悬在天际，

那里有紫色的葡萄累累垂垂，
高贵的骑士和美丽的女子
骑马从街道上走过。

啊！他们说，如果我能站在
那大山的山脊之上，
我看见的只能是大山两边
单调的田野和灰扑扑的树篱；
可是我知道我那神话的国土
就在那些树篱外面的某处。

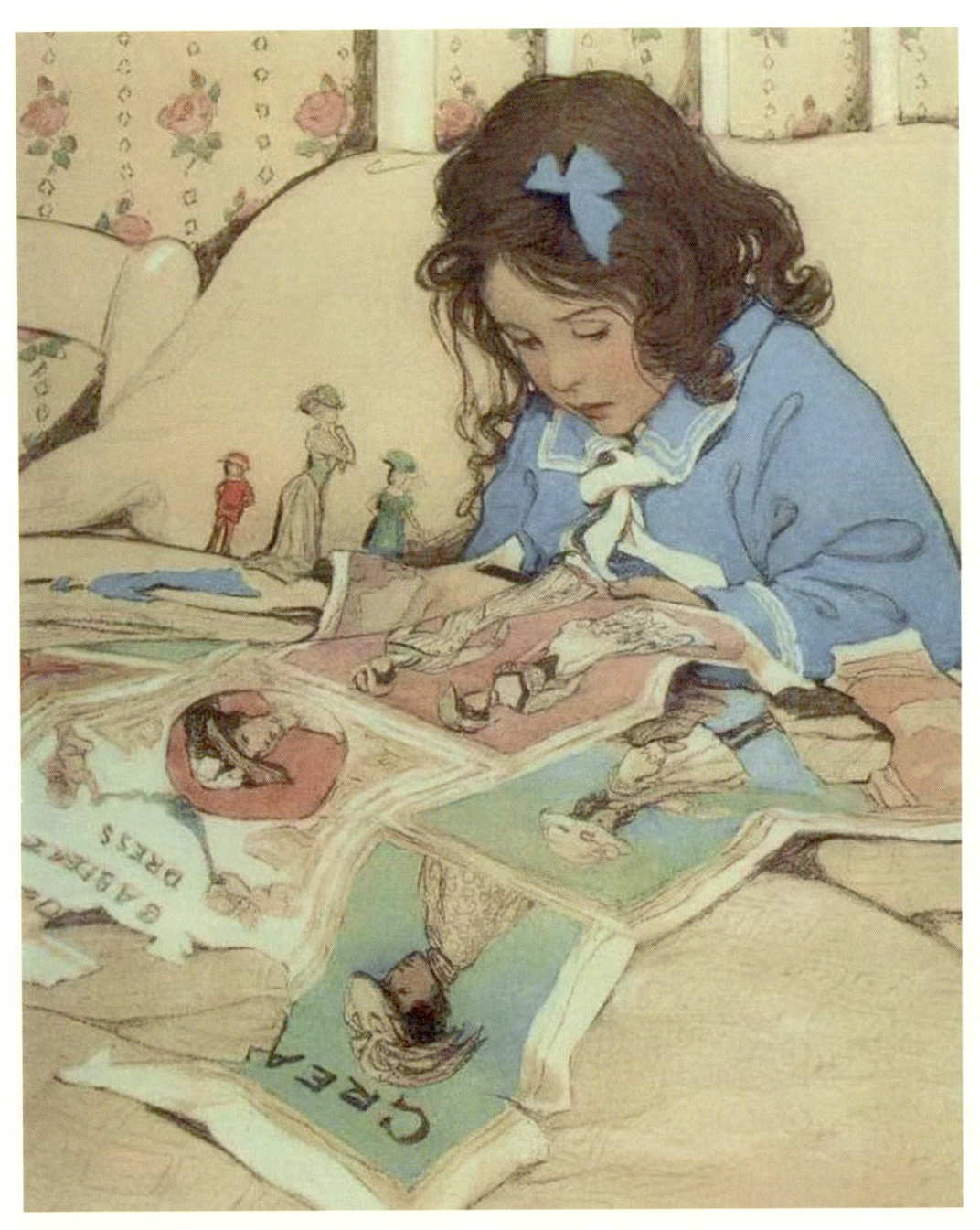

杰西·威尔科克斯·史密斯 绘

我的影子

罗伯特·路易斯·斯蒂文森

我有一个小影子随我进进出出,
我不明白他能有什么用处。
他从头到脚都和我很像,很像;
每次我要睡觉,他总是抢先跳上床。

他长大的样子,那才叫好玩——
一点不像平常小孩,总是长得很慢;
他有时像个橡皮球突然蹿高,
有时又缩得很小,根本看不到。

小孩该怎么游戏,他压根儿不懂,
只会想方设法,处处把我捉弄。
他紧紧地粘着我,看他有多胆小;
就像我粘着保姆,真是让人害臊!

有天一大早,太阳还没有露面,
我起床发现,金凤花上有露珠闪闪;
可我那懒惰的小影子,像个十足的懒鬼,
留在后面,赖在家里,呼呼大睡。

温斯洛·霍默 绘

每当我看见天上的彩虹

威廉·华兹华斯

每当我看见天上的彩虹
我的心就会狂跳不已:
在我生命之初就是这样;
现在长大成人还是这样;
当我年迈之时,也依然会这样,
否则,还不如让我死掉!
儿童乃是成人之父;
我期望自己未来的时日
能以自然的虔诚紧系在一起。

亨利·卢梭 绘

一个赤脚奔跑的婴儿

戴维·赫伯特·劳伦斯

当婴儿的赤脚敲打着穿过草地，
白色的小脚像花朵在风中点头，
它们跑跑停停，像涟漪在水面扩散；
看到这双白皙的脚在草间嬉戏，
就像知更鸟的歌声，那么迷人，
就像两只白蝴蝶，在一朵花的花萼中
安顿了片刻，又拍翅飞走。

我渴望这婴儿向我奔来，
就像风的影子在水面逡巡，
这样她就能站在我的膝上，
赤裸的小脚放在我的手中，
清凉如同丁香花的蓓蕾，
坚实柔润如同粉红初绽的牡丹。

杰西·威尔科克斯·史密斯 绘

第二辑 生灵

扬·范·戈因 绘

蝈蝈和蟋蟀

约翰·济慈

大地的诗歌永不消亡:
当炎炎烈日把百鸟晒晕,
藏进凉爽的树间,有一种声音
却在新割草场旁的篱笆间飘荡;

那是蝈蝈的嗓音。他带头歌唱,
在奢华的夏日;他的欢欣
永无止期,当他兴头已尽,

就去怡人的草叶下安歇。

大地的诗歌永不终止:
在孤独的冬夜,当严霜
冻出一片寂静,从炉边
响起蟋蟀尖声的吟唱,而炉火渐暖,
那睡意蒙眬的人恍惚又听见,
是蝈蝈歌唱在绿草茸茸的山间。

亨利·卢梭 绘

母牛

罗伯特·路易斯·斯蒂文森

温顺的母牛又红又白,
我毫无保留,爱她全心全意;
她尽力将奶油贡献,
让我就着苹果馅饼吃。

她哞哞叫着到处游逛,
却从来不会迷失,
怡人的白昼的阳光,
怡人的户外的空气;

所有的风都吹着她,
所有的雨都淋着她,
她在草场上漫步,
享受盛开的花。

温斯洛·霍默 绘

苍蝇

威廉·布莱克

小苍蝇，
你夏天的游戏
被我无心之手
轻轻拂去。

我不就是一只
和你一样的苍蝇？
你不也是一个
和我一样的人？

因为我跳舞，
喝水，歌唱，

直到一只盲目的手
拂去我的翅膀。

如果思想是生命，
是力量和呼吸，
那思想的匮乏
便是死亡；

那就是我，
一只幸福的苍蝇，
即便我活，
即便我死。

杰西·威尔科克斯·史密斯 绘

小羊羔

威廉·布莱克

小羊羔,是谁造了你?
你可知道是谁造了你?
给你生命,将你喂养
在溪水旁,在草地上;
给你衣服,让你高兴,
漂亮,柔软,毛茸茸;
给你如此温柔的嗓音,
使所有的山谷为之欢欣?
小羊羔,是谁造了你?
你可知道是谁造了你?

小羊羔,我要告诉你,
小羊羔,我要告诉你:
他以你的名为名,
他称自己是一只羔羊。
他又温顺,又谦恭,
他成了一个小小的孩童。
你是羔羊,我是孩童,
我们都以他的名为名。
小羊羔,上帝祝福你!
小羊羔,上帝祝福你!

利拉·卡博特·佩里 绘

老虎

威廉·布莱克

老虎，老虎，灿烂辉煌
熊熊燃烧，在黑夜的丛莽，
是什么样不朽的手和眼睛
能造就你这可怕的匀称？

在什么样遥远的海底天边，
燃烧起你眼中的火焰？
他凭借什么样的翅膀敢于凌空，
什么样的手敢于攫取这火种？

什么样的肩膀，什么样的技巧
才能拧成你心脏的筋肉？
而当你的心开始了跳跃，
什么样可怕的手，可怕的脚？

什么样的铁锤？什么样的铁链？
什么样的熔炉将你的头脑冶炼？
什么样的铁砧？什么样可怕的握力
竟敢死死抓住这些恐怖的东西？

当群星投下万道光芒，
又用泪水润湿了苍穹，
他可曾看着他的杰作微笑？
岂不是造了羔羊的他也将你创造？

老虎，老虎，灿烂辉煌
熊熊燃烧，在黑夜的丛莽，
是什么样不朽的手和眼睛
能造就你这可怕的匀称？

亨利·卢梭 绘

田鼠

塞西尔·弗朗西斯·亚历山大

在橡子滚落的地方,
白蜡树抖落它的浆果,
你的皮毛柔软棕黄,
你的眼睛又圆又快活,
深草几乎不会摇动,
田鼠,我能看见你从中经过。

小家伙,在什么黑暗的巢穴,
你整个冬天都呼呼大睡?
直到温暖的天气来临,
那时我会再次看见你
绕着大树根探头探脑,
啃咬它们掉落的果实。

田鼠,田鼠,你可别走,
农夫藏匿宝藏的所在
能找到掉落的坚果,
吃你的橡子吧,尽情开怀,
你没必要偷人家稻谷,
他囤积起来可是颇费踌躇。

在苔藓发芽之处掘土打洞,
在高大橡树的阴影下,
无害的东西,漂亮又安静,
在阳光和煦的草坪自在玩耍。
远离玉米和人类的房屋,
小田鼠,你就不会受到伤害。

温斯洛·霍默 绘

致蝴蝶

威廉·华兹华斯

我足足观察了你半个小时,
你静止在那朵黄花上,
还有,小蝴蝶!我真的不知
你是否睡觉,是否进食。
多静啊!——不是冰海
却要更静!那么好吧,
是什么欢乐在等你,当微风
在林中把你发现,
并再次呼唤你前往!

这片果园属于我们;
我的树,我妹妹的花。
在此歇下你疲倦的翅膀;
这住处仿若避难的天堂!
常来吧,别担心犯错;
和我们紧挨着坐在大树枝上!
我们将谈起阳光和歌曲,
还有我们年轻时的夏季;
甜蜜的童年,每一天
都和现在的二十天一样悠长。

杰西·威尔科克斯·史密斯 绘

鹰

阿尔弗雷德·丁尼生

他用弯曲的利爪攫住巉岩：
在孤独的大地上靠近太阳，
周遭是蔚蓝的世界，他静静伫立。

起皱的大海在他下面匍匐；
他从大山的围墙向下俯视，
然后像一声霹雳一掠而下。

亨利·卢梭 绘

猫头鹰

阿尔弗雷德·丁尼生

猫儿回家曙光出现,
寒露滴落大地,
远处激流默然无声,
风帆往来不息,
风帆往来不息;
温暖独坐气定神闲,
高高钟楼栖白鹰。

欢乐女工走进奶房,
细嗅新草香,
茅下公鸡啼声响亮,
两遍三遍回旋,
两遍三遍回旋;
温暖独坐气定神闲,
高高钟楼栖白鹰。

亨利·卢梭 绘

蜂鸟

戴维·赫伯特·劳伦斯

我可以想象，在另一个
原始无声，遥远的过去世界，
在那最为可怕的静止中，只有喘息嗡鸣的蜂鸟，
竞相飞过林荫道。

在事物拥有灵魂之前，
当生命还是一堆物质，只具有一半的生命，
这小小的一片，从光明中剥离下来，
从缓慢、巨大、肉质植物的茎秆间嗖嗖穿过。

我相信那里没有花，那时
世界上只有蜂鸟在创造之前闪耀着。
我相信他用长嘴刺穿迟钝的植物叶脉。

也许他很大，
就像苔藓，小蜥蜴，他们曾经都很大。
也许他是一个到处刺戳着的，可怕的怪物。

我们通过时间望远镜颠倒的一端观察他，
我们足够幸运。

亨利·卢梭 绘

鸭子的小调

肯尼斯·格雷厄姆

沿着一处荒僻的所在,
穿过高高的灯芯草,
鸭子们正在嬉戏。
全都尾巴朝上!

母鸭的尾巴,公鸭的尾巴,
黄色的脚在颤抖,
黄色的嘴完全看不见
在河中忙碌!

泥泞的绿色水草
有斜齿鳊在游泳——

这里是我们的食品室,
凉爽、丰富、幽暗。

人各有所爱!
我们喜欢
大头朝下,翘起尾巴,
自由地戏水!

在高高的蓝天上,
雨燕盘旋,呼唤——
我们在戏水,
尾巴全都朝上!

卡尔·朱兹 绘

两只小猫

珍·泰勒

一个暴风雪的晚上,
两只小猫,
吵了起来,
然后打成了一团。

其中一只有个老鼠,
另一只什么都没有;
就是因为这个,
它们吵了起来。

"老鼠得归我,"
大一点的小猫说。
"你想要老鼠?
我们走着瞧!"

"老鼠得归我,"

大猫乌龟壳说道;
然后,扑到妹妹身上,
又是吐口水,又是挠。

我以前和你说过,
那是一个暴风雪的夜晚,
两只小猫
打了起来。

老妇人拿起扫帚
来把房间打扫,
又把它们两个
全都扫地出门。

地上覆盖着
严霜和白雪,

它们失去了老鼠,
又无处可去。

于是,它们在地上发抖,
躺在门边,
直到老妇人
扫完了地板。

它们才溜进来,
安静得像老鼠,
全身都被雪打湿,
冷得像冰块。

它们终于发现,
暴风雪的夜晚,
躺在火炉旁边,
可比吵吵闹闹好得多。

亨利艾特·罗纳·克尼普 绘

蜘蛛

珍·泰勒

"噢，看那只丑陋的大蜘蛛！"
安妮尖叫着，用扇子把它撑开；
"这黑色的生灵还是那么吓人，
我可不想让它爬到我身上来。"

"是啊，"安妮的母亲说道，"我敢说，
这可怜的东西会设法避开你；
因为受了惊吓、坠落和痛苦，
它比你更有理由抱怨。

"可为什么你要害怕可怜的昆虫，亲爱的？
如果它伤害了你，你当然有理由害怕；
可它小小的黑腿，在它匆忙离开时，
我敢说，只会让你的胳膊有点发痒。

"它们害怕我们，这是理所应当，
我们瞬间就能把它们踏成齑粉；
我们当然没有任何理由恐慌；
它们无论如何，也伤害不到我们分毫。

"现在看！它已经回到了家；你没看见
它在树上织了一张精致纤细的网吗？
亲爱的安妮，这是给你准备的功课：
向蜘蛛学习忍耐的功夫！

"当你做事时却忍不住想要玩耍，
就回忆一下今天的这只小昆虫，
否则，你会羞愧难当，似乎
一只可怜的小蜘蛛都要比你聪明。"

约翰·乔治·伍德 绘

一只小鸟沿小径走来

艾米莉·狄金森

一只小鸟沿小径走来——
他不知道我看见了他——
他把一条蚯蚓啄成两段,
接着把这家伙活活吃掉,

然后他喝了一滴露水,
从一片就近的草叶上,
又侧身跳到路边的墙下
让一只甲虫通过——

他用滴溜溜乱转的眼睛
迅速地环视了左右——

他们就像受了惊吓的珠子,
抖了抖天鹅绒般的头

像遇险者一样小心翼翼,
我给了他一点面包屑,
他却展开翅膀
划了回去,轻快——

胜过分开海洋的船桨,
划出的缝隙更显得银白——
胜过蝴蝶从午时的岸边跃起,
游泳,却没有激起一丝浪花。

温斯洛·霍默 绘

草丛中一个细长的家伙

艾米莉·狄金森

草丛中一个细长的家伙
偶尔滑过去;
你也许遇见过——难道没有?
它的出现往往很突然。

草丛像被梳子分开,
一根带斑点的箭杆出现;
等草丛在你的脚边合拢,
更远处的草丛又分开。

它喜欢沼泽地,
那里冷得不生谷物。
当我还是个孩子,光着脚,
不止一次,在正午

与之相遇,我以为是鞭梢
散开在阳光下,
我正要弯腰拾起,
它却皱起身子,离开了。

我熟悉一些大自然的人士,
它们和我也十分要好;
我常常因为它们
感受到一种热诚的狂喜;

可每逢遇见这个家伙,
无论是有伴儿,还是独自一人,
我总是立刻呼吸发紧,
浑身冰冷,透入骨髓。

亨利·卢梭 绘

猫和月亮

威廉·巴特勒·叶芝

那猫儿走来走去,
那月亮如陀螺旋转,
月亮最近的亲戚,
那匍匐的猫,向上仰望。
黑猫米纳娄舍盯着月亮,
因为,当他漫游号叫,
天空中纯净的冷光
搅扰了他的兽性之血。
米纳娄舍在草间奔跑,
抬起他纤巧的脚。
你跳舞吗?米纳娄舍,跳舞吗?
两个近亲遇到一起,
还有什么比跳舞更好?
也许月亮厌倦了

那一套宫廷时尚,
会学习一种新的舞步。
米纳娄舍在草间潜行,
从一处到另一处月照之地,
头上神圣的月亮
已换了新的月相。
米纳娄舍可知否,他的瞳仁
将变了又变,
从圆到缺,
从缺到圆,周而复始?
米纳娄舍在草间潜行,
孤独,傲慢,聪明。
向变化着的月亮抬起
他变化着的眼睛。

埃罗·耶内费尔特 绘

小蜜蜂何其忙碌

艾萨克·瓦茨

小蜜蜂何其忙碌，
改善每个闪光的时辰，
整日收集甘蜜，
从每一朵盛开的花上！

她建筑蜂巢何其巧妙！
她铺展蜂蜡何其整洁！
辛勤劳作，存储稳妥，
用她创造的甜蜜。

无论是苦干还是巧干，
我也要同样忙碌；
因为撒旦会让无所事事的手
做出伤人的恶作剧。

在书中，工作中，或是健康的游戏中，
让我把最初的年月度过，
那样我就能为每一天
最终赋予美好的理由。

杰西·威尔科克斯·史密斯 绘

温斯洛·霍默 绘

鹰的嬉戏

沃尔特·惠特曼

沿着河边大道而行时,(我的午前散步,我的休息,)
天空中突然传来低沉的一声,是鹰的嬉戏,
是高空中迅疾的爱的接触,
利爪互相锁紧在一起,像一个活的、猛烈旋转的轮子,
四只拍击的翅膀,两个弯嘴,紧紧扭成旋转的一团,
翻着筋斗,转动一连串的圈子,笔直下坠,
直到接近河面才稳住,两个仍为一体,平静了片刻,
静止无声地在空中保持平衡,然后分开,松开利爪,
再次向上展开缓慢坚定的翅膀,倾斜着,各自飞行,
她有她的目的,他有他的追求。

一只沉默而坚忍的蜘蛛

沃尔特·惠特曼

一只沉默而坚忍的蜘蛛,
我注意到它孤独地站在一个小小的海岬上,
注意到它如何探索空阔的四周,
它从自己体内射出一缕,一缕,又一缕的蛛丝,
不断地抽出丝来,不知疲倦地加快速度。

而你,啊,我的灵魂,你站立之处,
被无数空间的海洋所环绕、隔离,
你不停地沉思、冒险、抛掷,寻找把海洋连接起来的领域;
直到你所需要的桥梁成形,直到柔韧的锚定住,
直到你抛出的游丝挂在某个地方,啊,我的灵魂。

杰西·威尔科克斯·史密斯 绘

第三辑　世界

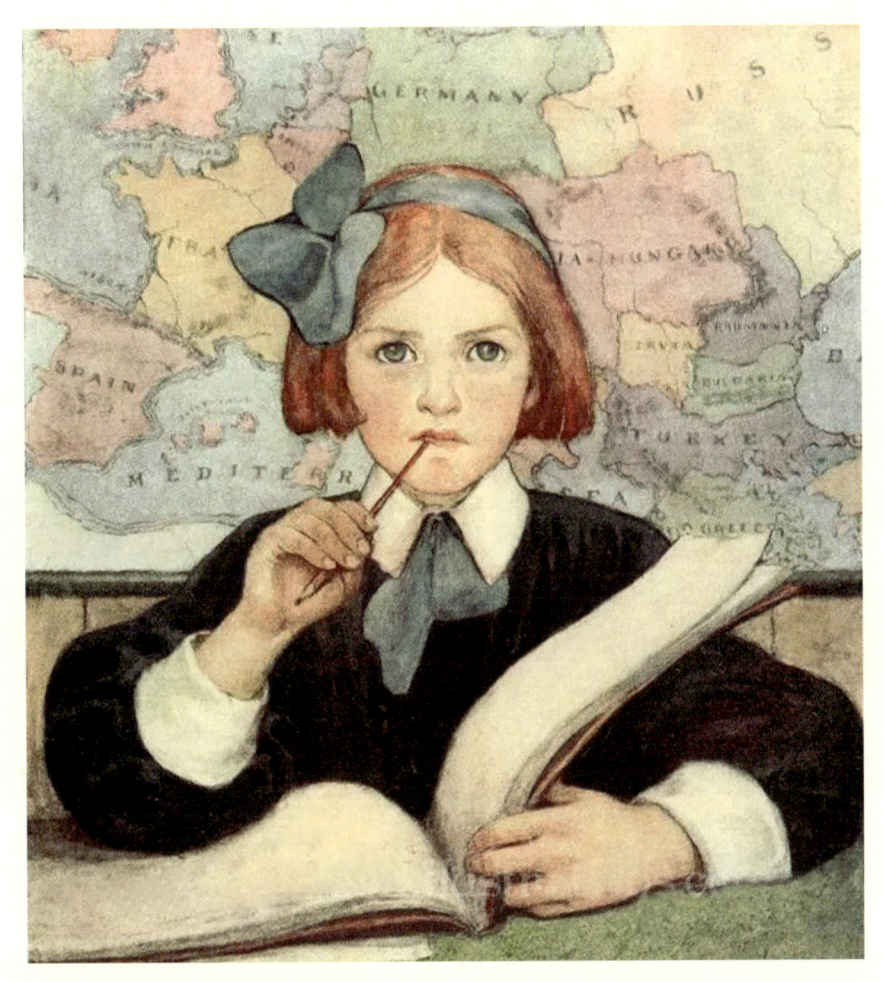

杰西·威尔科克斯·史密斯 绘

温斯洛·霍默 绘

希望是带羽毛的东西

艾米莉·狄金森

希望是带羽毛的东西,
栖息在灵魂中,
唱着无词的曲调,
从不会完全停息,

在暴风中听起来最为甜蜜;
暴风一定很是恼火,
它能让那温暖众人的小鸟
困窘不安。

我曾在最寒冷的陆地,
在最陌生的海上听到它;
但是,在绝境中,它也从不向我
索取些微的面包。

埃德温·奥斯汀·艾比 绘

我是无名之辈！你是谁？
艾米莉·狄金森

我是无名之辈！你是谁？
难道，你也是无名之辈？
那么我们就是一对儿了——不要说话！
他们会放逐我们，你知道。

多么厌倦，做一个某某！
多么出名，仿佛有一只青蛙
整天都在说着你的名字
对着一片钦慕的沼泽！

没有一艘快船能像一本书

艾米莉·狄金森

没有一艘快船能像一本书
载我们游历异乡,
也没有一匹骏马比得上
一页欢腾的诗章。

这是穷苦人都能完成的旅行,
没有通行税让他忧烦;
那运载灵魂的战车
是何等的节俭!

杰西·威尔科克斯·史密斯 绘

雪

菲利普·爱德华·托马斯

在白茫茫的阴郁中,
在雪的巨大沉默中,
一个孩子在痛苦地叹息:
"啊,一只白鸟被杀死在巢里,
她胸前的羽毛还在飘动!"
羽毛还在朦胧的光中坠落,
落在为那雪中的鸟儿哭泣的孩子身上。

马科斯菲尔德·帕里斯 绘

回答一个孩子的问题

塞缪尔·泰勒·柯勒律治

你问鸟儿们在说什么？麻雀，画眉，
鸽子和红雀说："我爱，我爱！"
冬天它们沉默了，风是如此猛烈；
风的话我不懂，它唱了一支响亮的歌。
可是绿叶，鲜花，明媚温暖的季节，
歌唱和爱都会结伴归来。
还有云雀，爱和欢乐溢满心田，
在蓝天和绿野之间，
唱着，唱着，它永远歌唱着——
"我爱我的爱，我的爱也爱我。"

马科斯菲尔德·帕里斯 绘

致水仙

罗伯特·赫里克

美丽的水仙,我们哭泣着看见
你匆匆而去,如此仓促;
如同早上升起的太阳
还没有抵达自己的正午。
且慢,且慢,
直到匆忙的时间
流逝,
却留下对等的歌曲;
我们一起祈祷,我们
和你同去。

我们短暂地停留,和你一样,
我们的春天同样地匆忙;
迅速成长,旋即腐朽。
和你,和万物一样。
我们死灭
如同你的时日,凋落和枯萎,
如同夏天的雨水;
如同晨露的珍珠,
一去不回。

亨利·卢梭 绘

秋天的火焰

罗伯特·路易斯·斯蒂文森

在另外的花园里,
在溪谷的上方,
秋天的篝火
有烟雾飘荡!

怡人的夏天过去,
还有所有夏天的花朵,
红色的火焰燃烧,
灰色的烟雾缭绕。
唱一首季节之歌!
万物都在闪耀!
夏天的花朵,
秋天的火焰!

马科斯菲尔德·帕里斯 绘

大风夜

罗伯特·路易斯·斯蒂文森

每当星月沉落,
每当风声正高,
长夜漫漫,黑暗潮湿,
一个人策马奔驰。
在炉火熄灭的深夜,
他为何奔驰又奔驰?

每当树木悲号,
船只在海上颠簸,
低身策马,蹄声响亮,
他在大路上驰过。
他奔驰而过,然后
又奔驰而回。

詹姆斯·盖尔·泰勒 绘

燧石

克里斯蒂娜·吉奥尔吉娜·罗塞蒂

绿宝石绿得像青草,
红宝石红得像血液;
蓝宝石闪亮,蓝得像天空;
燧石躺在淤泥里。

钻石是一块璀璨的石头,
捕捉住世界的欲望;
猫眼石留住一闪热烈的火花;
燧石留住的却是火焰。

杰西·威尔科克斯·史密斯 绘

顿悟

但丁·加百利·罗塞蒂

我曾经到过这里,
那是何时,何故,我无从断定;
我熟悉门外的青草,
甜蜜强烈的芳香,
围绕岸边的闪光和阵阵叹息。

你曾经属于我——
我不知那是多久以前;
但就在那飞燕翱翔之际,

你蓦然回首,
纱巾掉落——这一切我早就知晓。

莫非从前真的是这样?
时间的飞驰会不会再一次
复活我们的生活,我们的爱情
蔑视死亡,
日日夜夜再一次给予我们欢欣?

温斯洛·霍默 绘

我

沃尔特·德·拉·梅尔

只要我活着,
我就始终是
我自己——不是别人,
只是我自己。

就像一棵树——
柳树,接骨木,
山杨,荆棘,
或是被遗弃的柏树。

就像一朵花,
有自己的时辰——

报春花,或石竹花,
或是一朵紫罗兰——
被阳光照亮,
被雨露滋润。

始终只是我自己。
直到有一天
我离开这个身体,
那时一切都已结束,
身体里的灵魂
已经离去。

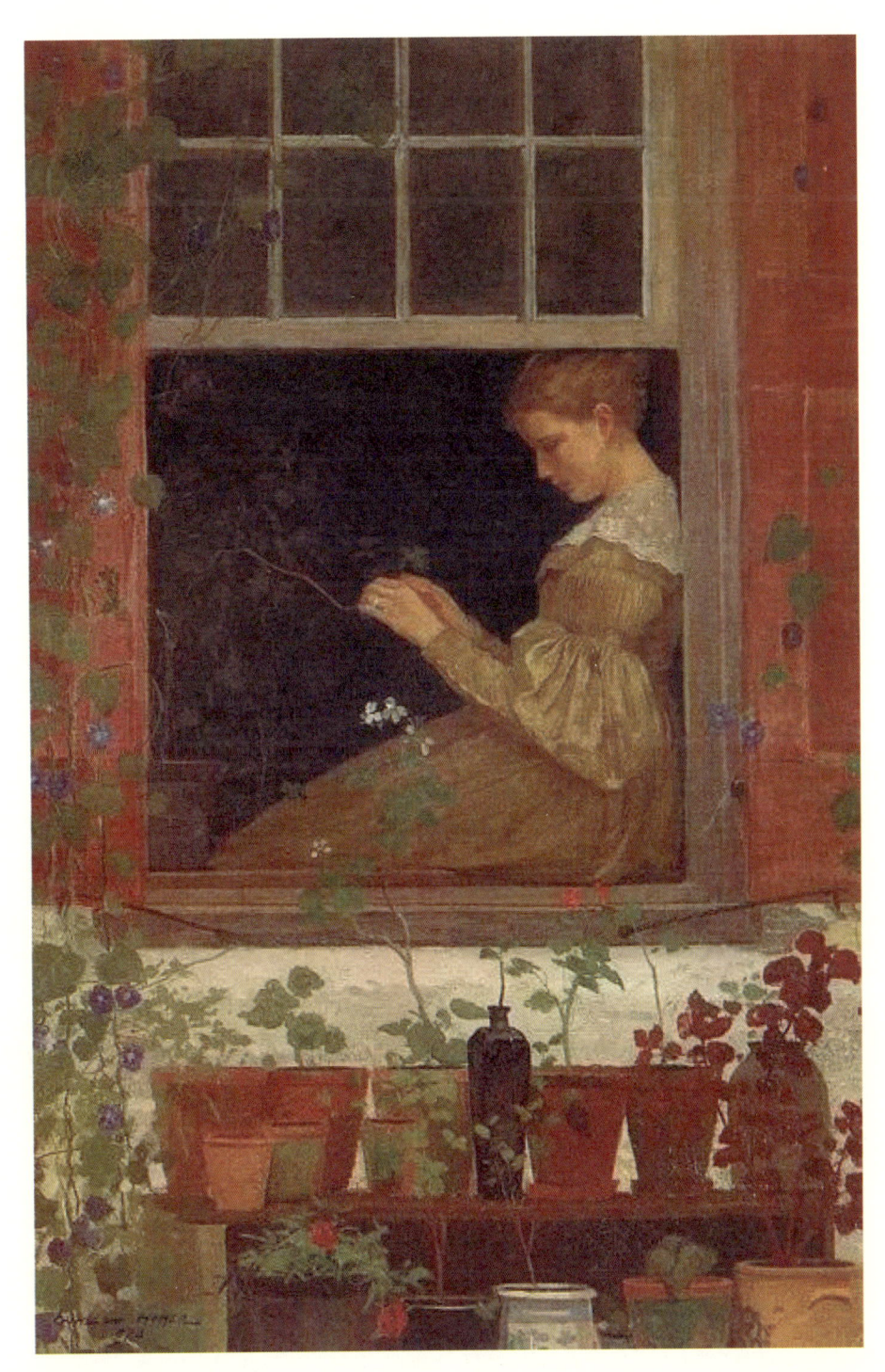

温斯洛·霍默 绘

诗人的歌

阿尔弗雷德·丁尼生

雨落了下来,诗人起身出门,
他绕过城市,离开街巷;
一阵微风从太阳之门吹来,
阴影的波浪漫过麦田;
他在一个僻静之处坐下,
唱出一支响亮又甜蜜的歌曲,
歌声让野天鹅停在云端,
让云雀飞落在他的脚边。

燕子忘记了捕捉苍蝇,
蛇悄悄滑到水沫下面。
老鹰伫立,嘴上粘着绒毛,
定睛凝视,爪子按住猎物;
而夜莺心想:"我整天歌唱,
但没有一支像这般欢欣,
因为他唱出了世界的真相
当岁月的纪年已湮没无踪。"

亨利·卢梭 绘

万物明亮又美丽

塞西尔·弗朗西斯·亚历山大

万物明亮又美丽,
世间生灵大大小小,
万物聪明又奇异,
万能上帝来创造。

一朵朵绽放的小花,
一只只歌唱的小鸟,
他造了它们绚丽的色彩,
也造了它们小小的翅膀。

紫色山顶的丘岗,
奔腾而过的河流,
日落和朝晖
照亮了天空。

冬天刺骨的冷风,
夏日怡人的阳光,
园中成熟的水果,
一切都是他的杰作。

他给我们眼睛能看,
他给我们会说话的嘴巴,
上帝何其伟大,
创造万物尽皆美好。

查尔斯·马里恩·拉塞尔 绘

咒语

艾米莉·勃朗特

周围的夜色在加深,
狂风冷冷地吹;
一个暴君的咒语将我束缚,
我不能,也不会离开。

巨人般的树弯下身,
积雪压满光秃的树枝。
风暴很快就会降临,
可我不会离开。

头上云彩叠着云彩,
下面荒原接着荒原;
但我不为任何恐惧所动,
我不愿,也不会离开。

迪恩·康威尔 绘

黄金国度

埃德加·爱伦·坡

一身华丽的服饰,
勇敢的骑士,
历经漫漫长途,
在阳光和阴影中奔驰,
唱着歌曲,
寻找黄金国度。

年华流逝——
这勇敢的骑士——
阴影罩上心头,
当他发现
没有任何地点
像似那黄金国度。

终于有一天
他年老力衰,
遇见了一个朝圣的影子——
"影子啊,"他说,
"这黄金国度
究竟在哪里?"

"在月亮上面,
群山那边,
在深深的影子谷,
奔驰吧,勇敢地奔驰,"
影子回答道——
"如果你要寻找黄金国度!"

迪恩·康威尔 绘

人的四季

约翰·济慈

四季的轮回充满一年的时光；
人的心灵也有四季分明：
他有旺盛的春天，让明朗的幻想
轻而易举地收纳，美的全部：

夏天降临，他喜欢用青春的思想
甜蜜地回味春天的奢华，
反复思量，让这高翔的梦
带他靠近天堂：
到了秋天，
他有宁静的小湾，这个时候
他紧紧地收拢翅膀，心满意足
悠闲地看着迷雾——让美的事物
像门前的小溪流过，不为人知。

他也有苍白的冬天，变了面目；
否则，便是超越了他凡人的本性。

马科斯菲尔德·帕里斯 绘

花园围墙那边

依里诺尔·法吉恩

花园围墙那边
有看不见的孩子们在嬉戏,
有人抛过一只球来,
在一个美好的夏日。
我把飞过来的球接住,
仿佛它直接来自一只陌生的手,
玩着一个愉快的游戏,
那是一个人单独玩不了的游戏。

那是只漂亮的球,
带着金带和蓝星;
我把它在手中转动,
感到好奇,然后我把球
抛过了花园围墙,
可这个宝贝又弹了回来——
是有人把它接住了,
并发出一阵嘲笑的声音。

杰西·威尔科克斯·史密斯 绘

那是在很久以前

依里诺尔·法吉恩

我要告诉你,我记得的事儿吗?
那依然对我意义重大的事儿。
那是在很久以前。

我记得夏天一条满是灰尘的路,
一座山,一座老房子,还有一棵树,
你知道,

立在房子后面。我记得一个老妇人
戴着红披巾,膝上有一只灰猫
在树下哼唱。

她似乎是我能记得的最古老的东西。
而我那时也许还不到三岁。
那是在很久以前。

我在满是灰尘的路上蹒跚而行,我记得
老妇人如何越过篱笆望着我,
似乎知道

三岁是什么感觉,我记得,她召唤说:
"你喜欢覆盆子和奶油做茶点吗?"
我走到树下。

随着她的哼唱,猫儿咕噜咕噜,我记得
她怎样为我装了一盘子覆盆子和奶油,
在很久以前。

在我的记忆中,这样的覆盆子和奶油
我从来没有见过,直到今天
也没有见过,你知道。

而那几乎就是我能记得的一切，
房子，山，她膝上的灰猫，
她的红披巾，还有树，

还有覆盆子的滋味，我记得阳光的感觉，
还有过往存在的一切的气息，
在很久以前，

直到我再次记起，外面路上的炎热，
似乎为我准备的满是灰尘的长路
没有尽头，你知道。

那就是我能记得的最远的事儿了。
它也许对你意义不大。对我却意义重大。
然后我就长大了，你看看。

杰西·威尔科克斯·史密斯 绘

打哈欠

依里诺尔·法吉恩

有时——抱歉——可是有时,
有时,是的,有时我感到厌倦。
也许是因为我是个白痴;
也许是因为我被难倒了;

也许是因为天在下雨,
也许是因为天气很热,
也许是因为我吃得
太多,或者是吃得太少。

可是有时我忍不住要打哈欠,
(抱歉了!)整个早晨都是哈欠连连——
而当老师转过身去,背对我们,
也许她也在打哈欠。

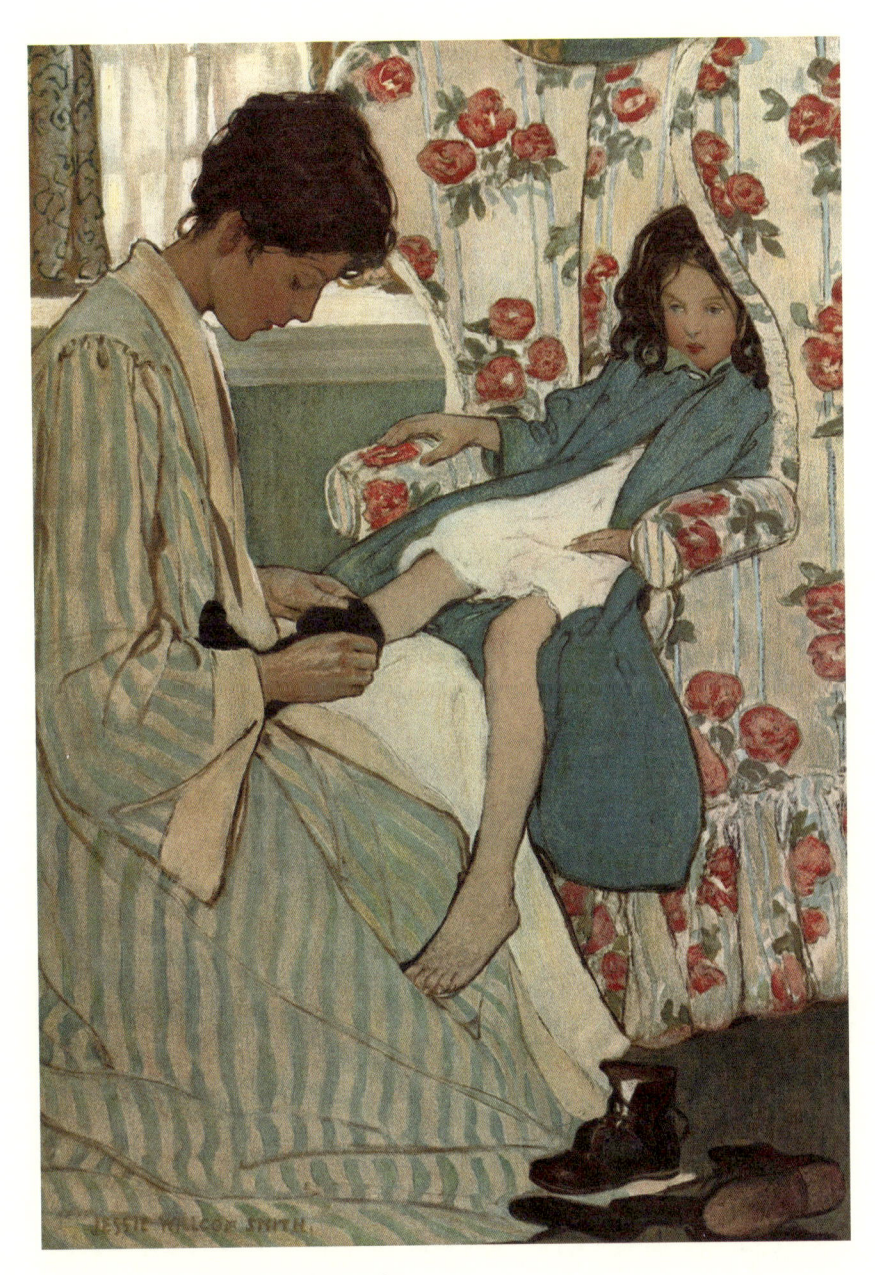

杰西·威尔科克斯·史密斯 绘

在下午的山岗上

埃德娜·圣·文森特·米莱

我将是太阳底下
最开心的人!
我将触摸一百朵鲜花
却一朵也不采摘。

我将注视悬崖和云彩
用宁静的眼睛,
观察风把草叶吹倒,
又重新立起。

而当镇上的灯光
开始亮起,
我将辨认哪一盏属于我,
然后起身下山!

哈维·邓恩 绘

未来

夏尔·克罗

马厩旁边成熟的干草里面
有黑罂粟和褪色的矢车菊,
我可敬的祖父那些发黄的书信,
满是对我祖母的老派誓言,

我大伯的鼻烟盒,
小桌上镶着的十五子的棋盘,
让我着迷,让我禁不住想象一个时代,
那时,我的诗也会让你着迷,而你尚未出生。

因为我确曾活过。每一阵风都带来
开花的山楂树和丁香的气息。
亲吻声淹没了慢腾腾的钟鸣。

哦,来吧读者,你将生活在十六岁的
欢乐、丁香花和初吻之中,
你的爱会让我腐烂的骨头欣喜不已。

温斯洛·霍默 绘

第四辑　自然及其他

马科斯菲尔德·帕里斯 绘

秋颂

约翰·济慈

雾气弥漫，果实圆熟的时日！
与成熟的太阳结成友伴；
密谋着如何用累累的果实
缀满茅屋檐下的葡萄藤蔓；
让苹果压弯屋前生苔的老树，
让果实一直熟透到心里；
使葫芦膨大，用甜蜜的果仁
丰满榛壳；又为蜜蜂
一次次催开晚花的蓓蕾，
让它们以为温暖的日子永不终结，
因为夏天已盈满黏稠的蜂巢。

谁不曾看见你经常在谷仓中央？
有时四处找找就能发现，
你散漫地坐在谷仓的地板上，
头发随簸谷的风轻轻忽闪；
或者酣睡在割了一半的垄沟里，
沉迷于罂粟花香，你的镰刀
放过了下一垄庄稼和缠绕的花；
有时像一个拾穗者穿过小溪，
挺着负重的头，稳健不晃摇；
或者在压榨机旁，几小时
耐心地守候，看浆汁慢慢地渗流。

啊！春天的歌在哪里？它们在哪里？
别去想它们吧——你有自己的音乐，
当条纹状的云催促白昼温柔地死去，
用玫瑰红抚摸残株散碎的田野；
这时，小蚊子的唱诗班
在河柳中悲悼，随微风起灭，
忽而上升，忽而下沉；
刚成年的小羊在多丘的小溪边高叫；
蟋蟀在树篱下歌唱，以柔和的高音，
一只知更雀在花园里呼哨；
成群的燕子在天空中啁啾不已。

亨利·卢梭 绘

多少诗人给时间的流逝镀上了金

约翰·济慈

多少诗人给时间的流逝镀上了金!
有几个向来是我的食粮,哺育
我喜悦的幻想——我可以沉思
它们的美丽,或是现实,或是崇高;
时常,当我坐下来安排诗韵,
这些诗章便蜂拥闯进我的脑海:
没有混乱,没有粗鲁的打扰,
却是一片和谐怡人的叮当。
傍晚就这样蕴藏无数的声响;
群鸟的歌唱——树叶的低语——
流水的声音——大钟发出
庄严的轰鸣,还有上千种音响,
遥远得难以分辨,它们构成一曲
美妙的音乐,而不是狂野的喧嚷。

埃德温·奥斯汀·艾比 绘

啊，孤独！如果我必须与你同住

约翰·济慈

啊，孤独！如果我必须与你同住，
不要住在乱糟糟昏暗的建筑
当中：请和我一起攀登陡坡，
去那大自然的瞭望台——俯瞰幽谷，
开满鲜花的山坡，河水如水晶，
似乎近在咫尺；让我守护着你
在枝叶的荫蔽下，看小鹿纵跃，
从毛地黄的花钟将野蜂惊飞。
尽管我愉快地伴你探寻美景，
可是同纯真心灵甜蜜的对话，
让词语成为思想精妙的形象，
是我灵魂的快事；而且定然如此
这几乎是人类最高的福分，
当两种相似的精神向你奔去。

埃德温·奥斯汀·艾比 绘

黄水仙

威廉·华兹华斯

我孤独地漫游,像一片云
高高地飘荡在山谷和峰峦,
突然间我看见一大片
金色的黄水仙,
开放在湖边,在树荫下,
迎着微风飘动和舞蹈。

连绵不断,如群星灿烂,
在银河里闪闪发光,
它们的队列无尽地延伸,
沿着湖湾的边缘;
我一眼就看见了千万朵,
在活泼的舞蹈中摇曳着花冠。

波浪也在它们身边舞蹈,
水仙的欢喜却胜过了粼粼水波:
有了这样快活伴侣,
诗人怎能不心旷神怡:
我久久凝视——却难以想到
这景象带给我怎样的财富:

从此,每当我倚榻而卧,
心境空茫,忧郁沉思,
它们便在我的心目之中闪现,
那是孤独之中的极乐;
于是我的心便充满了幸福,
与黄水仙一同翩然起舞。

亨利·卢梭 绘

啊，向日葵

威廉·布莱克

啊，向日葵！厌倦了时间，
你点数太阳的脚步；
追寻着那甜蜜的金色国度，
旅行者的行程在那里结束。

那里，因欲望而憔悴的少年，
身披白雪的苍白少女；
全都从他们的坟墓中起来，
渴望着我的向日葵要去的地方。

亨利·卢梭 绘

一片残雪

罗伯特·弗罗斯特

角落里有一片残雪,
我猜测
是雨水吹落的
一张报纸。

它布满了污点,好像
铺满小小的铅字,
是哪一天的新闻,我已忘记——
即便我曾经读过。

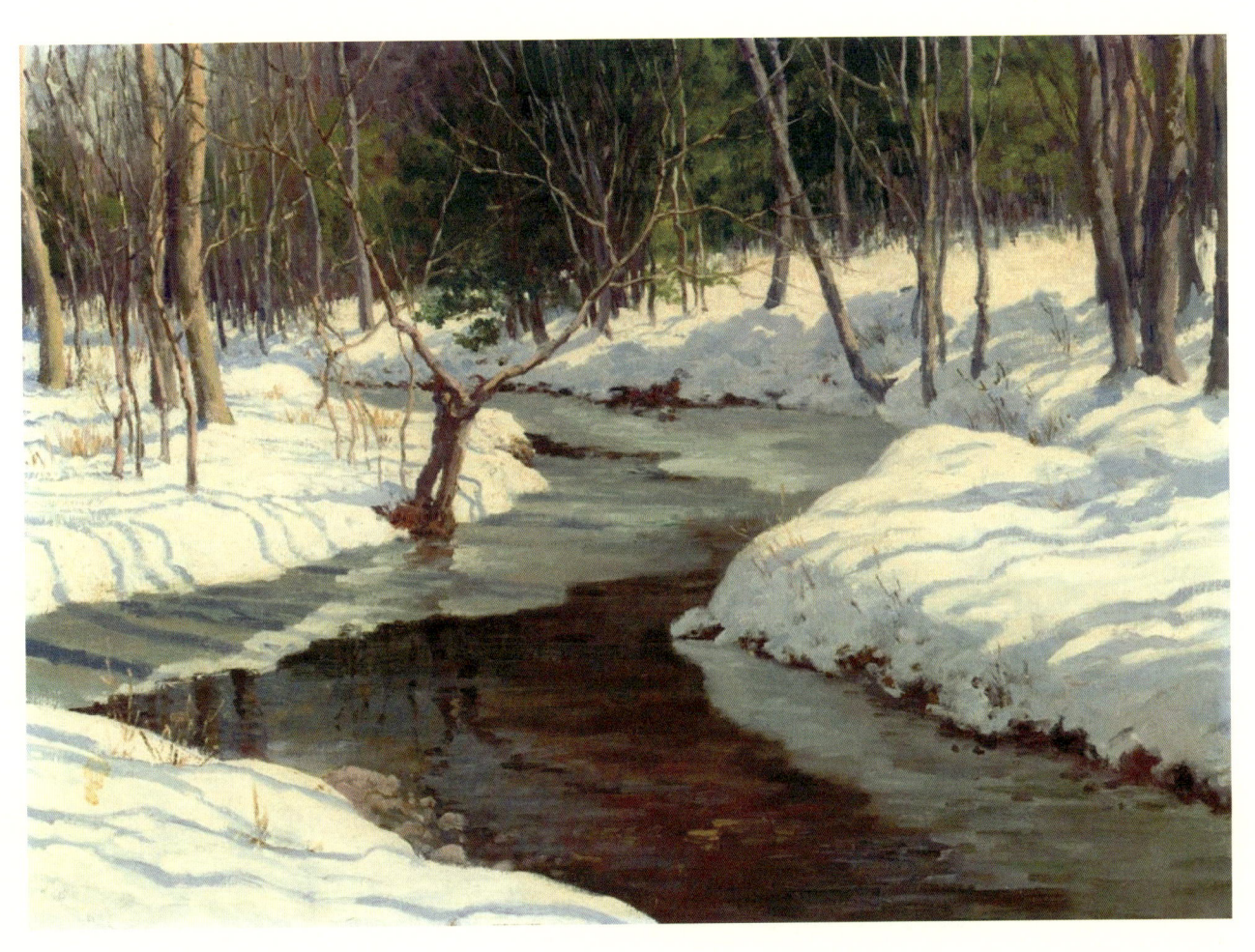

安东·奥托·菲舍尔 绘

未走的路

罗伯特·弗罗斯特

黄色的树林中有两条分岔的路，
可惜我不能同时把它们涉足。
作为一个旅人，我长久地伫立，
向其中一条极目远眺，
直到它转弯，消失在灌木丛中。

然后我选择了另外一条路线，
同样幽美，也许更合我意，
因为它芳草萋萋，无人践踏，
至于讲到来往行人的足迹，
两条路真的无甚差别。

那天清晨，两条路都埋在
落叶下面，还没有被脚步踩黑。
哦，我把第一条留待他日！
虽然知道，路与路相通，
我怀疑是否还能回到原处。

此后岁月经年，四处漂泊，
我将会叹息着向人们说起：
树林中有两条分岔的路，
而我——选择了人迹罕至的那条，
于是便有了这迥然相异的一切。

埃德温·奥斯汀·艾比 绘

雪夜林边驻足

罗伯特·弗罗斯特

我想我知道这是谁的林子。
他的房子虽在那边的村里；
他不会看见我在此停留，
伫望他的树林落满了白雪。

我的小马一定会觉得奇怪，
停留在荒无人烟的地方，
在树林和结冻的湖泊之间，
又是一年中最黑暗的夜晚。

它摇了摇马具上的铃铛，
问我是否出了什么差错。
此外唯一的声音
是掠过的风和柔软的雪片。

这树林真可爱，黑暗而深邃，
可是我还有诺言要遵守，
还有好几里路才能安歇。
还有好几里路才能安歇。

马科斯菲尔德·帕里斯 绘

茵尼斯弗利湖岛

威廉·巴特勒·叶芝

我就要启程,前往茵尼斯弗利,
用泥巴和板条,在那里造一座小屋:
种九排豆角,养一箱蜜蜂,
独居在蜜蜂嗡嘤的林间空地。

我将拥有些许安宁,安宁缓慢降临,
从清晨的面纱滴向蟋蟀歌唱的地方;
午夜微光粼粼,中午紫光闪耀,
傍晚充满红雀的翅膀。

我就要启程,因为每日每夜,
我总是听到湖水低声拍打着湖岸;
当我伫立在马路上,或是在灰色的人行道上,
我总是在内心深处听见它的召唤。

温斯洛·霍默 绘

美德

乔治·赫伯特

甜蜜的白天，如此凉爽、宁静、明媚，
那是大地和天空的婚礼；
但露水将哭泣你坠入夜晚，
因为你终必有死。

甜蜜的玫瑰，鲜艳怒放，勇敢非凡，
吩咐那草率的赏花人擦亮双眼；
你的根总是扎在花坟深处，
而你终必有死。

甜蜜的春天，充满甜蜜的白昼和玫瑰，
那是一个盒子，密密实实装满了甜美；
我的音乐显明你自有终局，
而一切都终必有死。

只有一个甜美而圣洁的灵魂，
如同风干的木材，永不放弃；
即便整个世界都化为焦炭，
它也会活着，永无止期。

乔治·莫兰 绘

本能

伊迪特·伊蕾内·索德格朗

我的身体是个谜。
只要这脆弱的东西活着,
你就能感到它的力量。
我将拯救世界。
因此爱神的血液通过我的嘴唇奔涌,
爱神的黄金进入我疲惫的卷发。
我只需要去看,
疲惫或者痛苦:世界是我的。
当我筋疲力尽地躺在床上,
我知道:在这虚弱的手中躺着世界的命运。
那是在我的鞋子里颤抖的力量,
那是在我衣褶里移动的力量,
那是站在你面前的力量,不惧怕深渊。

杰西·威尔科克斯·史密斯 绘

我童年的树木

伊迪特·伊蕾内·索德格朗

我童年的树木高高地立在草中
摇着头：你已经变成了什么？
成排的柱子立着，仿佛在责备：
你不配在我们下面散步！
你是个孩子，你应该知道一切，
为什么还被你的疾病所束缚？
你变成了一个人，陌生而讨厌。
在你小时，几小时地和我们交谈，
你有一双聪明的眼睛。
不，我们不想告诉你生活的秘密：
所有秘密的钥匙都躺在草中的悬钩子旁。
我们想把你摇醒，你这沉睡的人，
我们想唤醒你这麻木的人，从你的睡眠中。

温斯洛·霍默 绘

林中湖泊

伊迪特·伊蕾内·索德格朗

在阳光照耀的岸上,我独处
在林中灰蓝色的湖泊旁,
空中飘着一朵孤云,
水上漂着一座孤岛。
夏天成熟的甜蜜
从每棵树上的水珠中滴落,
径直落入我敞开的心里,
淌下小小的一滴。

托马斯·赖特 绘

星

伊迪特·伊蕾内·索德格朗

当黑暗降临,
我站在台阶上倾听;
星星拥挤在花园里,
我站在黑暗中。
倾听一颗星落地的声音!
你不要赤足在草地上散步,
我的花园满是星星的碎片。

马科斯菲尔德·帕里斯 绘

我看见路易斯安那有一棵橡树在生长

沃尔特·惠特曼

我看见路易斯安那有一棵橡树在生长,
它全然孤独地立着,苔藓从树枝上垂下来,
没有同伴,它在那里生长,倾吐出暗绿色的快乐,
而它的样貌,粗鲁、刚直、健壮,让我想起我自己,
但是我惊奇,它如何能够吐出快乐的叶子,独自站在那里,
近旁没有朋友,因为我清楚我做不到,
我折下一根嫩枝,上面带着一些树叶,给它绕上一点苔藓,
我把它带走,放在我房间看得见的地方,
它不需要使我重新想起我那些亲爱的朋友,
(因为我相信最近除了他们我很少想别的,)
然而它对我始终是一个奇异的记号,让我想起男子的爱;
虽然如此,虽然那橡树还在路易斯安那闪光,孤独地立在广阔又广阔的平地上,
倾吐着快乐的叶子,终生没有一个朋友、一个恋人在近旁,
我十分清楚我做不到。

巴伦德·阿普尔曼 绘

当我听到那博学的天文学家

沃尔特·惠特曼

当我听到那博学的天文学家；
当那些证明、数字在我面前排列成行；
当那些图表展示给我，还要增添、划分、测量；
当我坐着听见天文学家在讲堂里演讲且受到热烈喝彩，
我不久就变得莫名地疲惫和厌倦；
我起身溜出去，独自在外面徘徊，
在神秘湿润的夜气中，时不时地
在完全的寂静中仰望天上的群星。

温斯洛·霍默 绘

奇迹

沃尔特·惠特曼

唉,谁会重视一个奇迹呢?
至于我,除了奇迹我一无所知,
无论我是走在曼哈顿的街道,
或者让视线越过屋顶,投向天空,
或者赤着脚沿着海滩边涉水,
或者站在林中的树底下,
或者白天和任何一个我爱的人交谈,晚上和任何一个我爱的人同眠,
或者晚餐时和其他人坐在桌边,
或者乘车时看着我对面的陌生人,
或者夏日午前观察蜜蜂在蜂巢周围忙碌,
或者在田野里觅食的动物,
或者是鸟类,空气中飞虫的奇妙,
或者是日落的奇妙,如此宁静而明亮地闪耀的群星,
或者是春天的新月那精致优雅的纤细的弧形;
这些和其他,一和一切,对我都是奇迹,
都关乎整体,又各自独立,各从其位。

对我来说，光与暗的每一个时辰都是一个奇迹，

每一立方英寸的空间都是一个奇迹，

大地的每一平方码都铺展着同样的东西，

每一英尺之内都拥挤着同样的东西。

对我来说，大海是一个持续不断的奇迹，

游泳的鱼——岩石——波浪的运动——载人的船，

还有比它们更神奇的奇迹吗？

查尔斯·马里恩·拉塞尔 绘

记忆

托马斯·贝利·奥尔德里奇

我的心遗忘了上千件事情,
比如战争和国王驾崩的日期,
却记住了那一个时辰——
村里的钟楼,是正午时分,
五月最后一个晴朗的日子——
凉爽的清风活泼地吹起,
吹皱了路旁的那一条小溪;
然后,在这里停下,播撒
松树的香味,又从野玫瑰树上
懒懒地摇下两片花瓣。

温斯洛·霍默 绘

致水鸟

威廉·卡伦·布莱恩特

你要去往何方？露珠正在坠落,
天穹闪耀着白昼最后的脚步,
远远地,穿过玫瑰色的深处,
你求索着孤独的道路。

也许,猎鸟者的眼睛
徒劳地看着你远飞,想要伤害你,
当红色的天空衬着你的身影,
你飘摇而去。

你想要飞往何处?
要寻觅杂草丛生、潮湿的湖岸?
大河的边沿,还是磨损的海滩?
那里有动荡的巨浪起起落落。

有一种力量关照着你,
教导你在无路的海滨——
荒漠和浩渺的长空——
独自漫游,不会迷失。

你整天拍打着翅膀,
扇着远天那稀薄寒冷的大气,
尽管黑夜已靠近,你已疲惫,
也不肯屈尊降落安全的大地。

不久,那折磨就会结束;
不久,你就会找到夏天的家,歇下,
在同伴间欢叫;不久,
芦苇将弯下,在你隐蔽的巢上。

你消失了,天空的深渊
吞噬了你的身影;但在我心上
已深深留下你教给我的一课,
它不会很快就遗忘。

谁引导你穿过无垠的天空,
从一个领域到另一个领域,
也会在我必须独自跋涉的长途上,
正确地引导我的脚步。

安东·奥托·菲舍尔 绘

缪斯

安娜·安德烈耶夫娜·阿赫玛托娃

在夜里,我耐心地等待着她,
生命,似乎系于一发之间。
和这位手持长笛的亲爱的客人相比,
什么尊严、青春、自由,又算得了什么。

她终于来了,撩开了面纱,
严厉地俯视着我,我对她说:
"是你向但丁口授了《地狱篇》?"
她回答:"是的,是我。"

埃德温·奥斯汀·艾比 绘

我不与人争

沃尔特·萨维奇·兰多

我不与人争，也无人值得我争。
爱的是自然，其次是艺术；
生命之火前我温暖我的双手；
火光微弱了，我也准备离开。

温斯洛·霍默 绘

《和孩子一起读诗》

英文篇

Part One Childhood
第一辑 童年

一年的十二个月份
The Months of the Year

Sara Coleridge

January brings the snow,
makes our feet and fingers glow.

February brings the rain,
Thaws the frozen lake again.

March brings breezes loud and shrill,
stirs the dancing daffodil.

April brings the primrose sweet,
Scatters daises at our feet.

May brings flocks of pretty lambs,
Skipping by their fleecy damns.

June brings tulips, lilies, roses,
Fills the children's hand with posies.

Hot July brings cooling showers,
Apricots and gillyflowers.

August brings the sheaves of corn,
Then the harvest home is borne.

Warm September brings the fruit,
Sportsmen then begin to shoot.

Fresh October brings the pheasents,
Then to gather nuts is pleasent.

Dull November brings the blast,
Then the leaves are whirling fast.

Chill December brings the sleet,
Blazing fire, and Christmas treat.

兄妹俩

Brother and Sister

Lewis Carroll

"SISTER, sister, go to bed!
Go and rest your weary head."
Thus the prudent brother said.

"Do you want a battered hide,
Or scratches to your face applied?"
Thus his sister calm replied.

"Sister, do not raise my wrath.
I'd make you into mutton broth
As easily as kill a moth."

The sister raised her beaming eye
And looked on him indignantly
And sternly answered, "Only try!"

Off to the cook he quickly ran.
"Dear Cook, please lend a frying-pan
To me as quickly as you can."

"And wherefore should I lend it you?"
"The reason, Cook, is plain to view.
I wish to make an Irish stew."

"What meat is in that stew to go?"
"My sister'll be the contents!"
"Oh"
"You'll lend the pan to me, Cook?"
"No!"

Moral: Never stew your sister.

男孩之歌

A Boy's Song

James Hogg

Where the pools are bright and deep,
Where the grey trout lies asleep,
Up the river and over the lea,
That's the way for Billy and me.

Where the blackbird sings the latest,
Where the hawthorn blooms the sweetest,
Where the nestlings chirp and flee,
That's the way for Billy and me.

Where the mowers mow the cleanest,
Where the hay lies thick and greenest,
There to track the homeward bee,
That's the way for Billy and me.

Where the hazel bank is steepest,
Where the shadow falls the deepest,

Where the clustering nuts fall free,
That's the way for Billy and me.

Why the boys should drive away
Little sweet maidens from the play,
Or love to banter and fight so well,
That's the thing I never could tell.

But this I know, I love to play
Through the meadow, among the hay;
Up the water and over the lea,
That's the way for Billy and me.

独自
Alone

Edgar Allan Poe

From childhood's hour I have not been
As others were; I have not seen
As others saw; I could not bring
My passions from a common spring.
From the same source I have not taken
My sorrow; I could not awaken
My heart to joy at the same tone;
And all I loved, I loved alone.
Then—in my childhood, in the dawn
Of a most stormy life—was drawn
From every depth of good and ill
The mystery which binds me still:

From the torrent, or the fountain,
From the red cliff of the mountain,
From the sun that round me rolled
In its autumn tint of gold,
From the lightning in the sky
As it passed me flying by,
From the thunder and the storm,
And the cloud that took the form
(When the rest of Heaven was blue)
Of a demon in my view.

有个老头胡子长
There Was an Old Man with a Beard

Edward Lear

There was an old man with a beard,
Who said, "It is just as I feared!—
Two owls and a hen, four larks and a wren
Have all built their nests in my beard!"

奥西曼迪斯
Ozymandias

Percy Bysshe Shelley

I met a traveler from an antique land,
Who said—"Two vast and trunkless legs of stone

Stand in the desert..." Near them, on the sand,
Half sunk, a shattered visage lies, whose frown,
And wrinked lip, and sneer of cold command,
Tell that its sculptor well those passions read
Which yet survive, stamped on these lifeless things,
The hand that mocked them, and the heart, that fed;
And on the pedestal, these words appear:
"My name is Ozymandias, King of Kings,
Look on my works, ye Mighty, and despair!"
Nothing besides remains. Round the decay
Of that colossal Wreck, boundless and bare
The lone and level sands stretch faraway.

Echo on echo
Dies to the moon.

Two bright stars
Peeped into the shell.
"What are they dreaming of?
Who can tell?"

Startled a green linnet
Out of the croft;
Wake little ladies,
The sun is aloft!

明妮和温妮

Minnie and Winnie

Alfred Lord Tennyson

Minnie and Winnie
Slept in a shell.
Sleep little ladies!
And they slept well.

Pink was the shell within,
Silver without;
Sounds of the great sea
Wandered about.

Sleep little ladies,
Wake not soon!

老太婆麦格

Old Meg She Was a Gipsy

John Keats

Old Meg she was a gipsy,
And liv'd upon the moors;
Her bed it was the brown heath turf,
And her house was out of doors.

Her apples were swart blackberries,
Her currants pods o'broom;
Her wine was dew of the wild white rose,
Her book a churchyard tomb.

Her Brothers were the craggy hills,
Her Sisters larchen trees—

Alone with her great family
She live'd as she did please.

No breakfast had she many a morn,
No dinner many a noon,
And' stead of supper she would stare
Full hard against the Moon.

But every morn of woodbine fresh
She made her garlanding,
And every night the dark glen Yew
She wove, and she would sing.

And with her fingers old and brown
She plaited mats o' Rushes,
And gave them to the Cottagers
She met among the Bushes.

Old Meg was brave as Margaret Queen
And tall as Amazon:
An old red blanket cloak she wore;
A chip hat had she on.
God rest her aged bones somewhere—
She died full long agone!

给我的兄弟
To My Brothers

John Keats

Small, busy flames play through the fresh laid coals,
And their faint cracklings o'er our silence creep
Like whispers of the household gods that keep
A gentle empire o'er fraternal souls.
And while for rhymes I search around the poles,
Your eyes are fixed, as in poetic sleep,
Upon the lore so voluble and deep,
That aye at fall of night our care condoles.
This is your birth-day, Tom, and I rejoice
That thus it passes smoothly, quietly.
Many such eves of gently whispering noise
May we together pass, and calmly try
What are this world's true joys, ere the great Voice
From its fair face shall bid our spirits fly.

所有的钟都在鸣响
All The Bells Were Ringing

Christina Georgina Rossetti

All the bells were ringing,
And all the birds were singing,
When Molly sat down crying
For her broken doll:
O you silly Moll!
Sobbing and sighing
For a broken doll,
When all the bells are ringing
And all the bird are singing.

如果小猪戴假发
If a Pig Wore a Wig

Christina Georgina Rossetti

If a pig wore a wig,
What could we say?
Treat him as a gentleman,
And say "Good-day."

If his tail chanced to fall,
What could we do?
Send him to the tailoress
To get one new.

谁曾见过风？
Who Has Seen the Wind?

Christina Georgina Rossetti

Who has seen the wind?
Neither I nor you:
But when the leaves hang trembling,
The wind is passing through.

Who has seen the wind?
Neither you nor I:
But when the trees bow down their heads,
The wind is passing by.

微小的事物
Little Things

Julia Abigail Fletcher Carney

Little drops of water,
Little grains of sand,
Make the mighty ocean
And the beauteous land.

And the little moments,
Humble though they be,
Make the mighty ages
Of eternity.

So our little errors
Lead the soul away,
From the paths of virtue
Into sin to stray.

Little deeds of kindness,
Little words of love,
Make our earth an Eden,
Like the heaven above.

夜

Night

William Blake

The sun descending in the west,
The evening star does shine;
The birds are silent in their nest.
And I must seek for mine.
The moon, like a flower
In heaven's high bower,
With silent delight
Sits and smiles on the night.

Farewell, green fields and happy grove,
Where flocks have took delight:
Where lambs have nibbled, silent move
The feet of angels bright;
Unseen they pour blessing
And joy without ceasing
On each bud and blossom,
On each sleeping bosom.

They look in every thoughtless nest
Where birds are cover'd warm;
They visit caves of every beast,
to keep them all from harm:
If they see any weeping
That should have been sleeping,
They pour sleep on their head,
And sit down by their bed.

When wolves and tigers howl for prey,
They pitying stand and weep,
Seeking to drive their thirst away
And keep them from the sheep.
But, if they rush dreadful,
The angels, most heedful,
Receive each mild spirit,
New worlds to inherit.

And there the lion's ruddy eyes
Shall flow with tears of gold:
And pitying the tender cries,
And walking round the fold:
Saying, "Wrath by His meekness,
And, by His health, sickness,
Are driven away
From our immortal day."

"And now beside thee, bleating lamb,
I can lie down and sleep,
Or think on Him who bore thy name,
Graze after thee, and weep.
For, wash'd in life's river,
My bright mane for ever
Shall shine like the gold
As I guard o'er the fold."

一个梦

A Dream

William Blake

Once a dream did weave a shade
O'er my angel-guarded bed,
That an emmet lost its way
Where on grass methought I lay.

Troubled, wildered, and forlorn,
Dark, benighted, travel-worn,
Over many a tangled spray,
All heart-broke, I heard her say:

"O my children! do they cry,
Do they hear their father sigh?
Now they look abroad to see,
Now return and weep for me."

Pitying, I dropped a tear:
But I saw a glow-worm near,
Who replied, "What wailing wight
Calls the watchman of the night?

"I am set to light the ground,
While the beetle goes his round:
Follow now the beetle's hum;
Little wanderer, hie thee home!"

梦境

Dreams

Cecil Frances Alexander

Beyond, beyond the mountain line,
The grey-stone and the boulder,
Beyond the growth of dark green pine,
That crowns its western shoulder,
There lies that fairy land of mine,
Unseen of a beholder.

Its fruits are all like rubies rare,
Its streams are clear as glasses;
There golden castles hang in air,
And purple grapes in masses,
And noble knights and ladies fair
Come riding down the passes.

AH me! They say if I could stand
Upon those mountain ledges,
I should but see on either hand
Plain field and dusty hedges:
And yet I know my fairy land
Lies somewhere over their hedges.

我的影子

My Shadow

Robert Louis Stevenson

I have a little shadow that goes in and out with me,
And what can be the use of him is more than I can see.
He is very, very like me from the heels up to the head;
And I see him jump before me, when I jump into my bed.

The funniest thing about him is the way he likes to grow—
Not at all like proper children, which is always very slow;
For he sometimes shoots up taller like an india-rubber ball,
And he sometimes gets so little that there's none of him at all.

He hasn't got a notion of how children ought to play,
And can only make a fool of me in every sort of way.
He stays so close beside me, he's a coward you can see;
I'd think shame to stick to nursie as that shadow sticks to me!

One morning, very early, before the sun was up,
I rose and found the shining dew on every buttercup;
But my lazy little shadow, like an arrant sleepy-head,
Had stayed at home behind me and was fast asleep in bed.

每当我看见天上的彩虹

My Heart Leaps up When I Behold

William Wordsworth

My heart leaps up when I behold
A rainbow in the sky:
So was it when my life began;
So it is now I am a man;
So be it when I shall grow old,
Or let me die!
The child is father of the man;
And I could wish my days to be
Bound each to each by natural piety.

一个赤脚奔跑的婴儿

A Baby Running Barefoot

David Herbert Lawrence

When the bare feet of the baby beat across the grass
The little white feet nod like white flowers in the wind,
They poise and run like ripples lapping across the water;
And the sight of their white play among the grass
Is like a little robin's song, winsome,
Or as two white butterflies settle in the cup of one flower

For a moment, then away with a flutter of wings.

I long for the baby to wander hither to me
Like a wind-shadow wandering over the water,

So that she can stand on my knee
With her little bare feet in my hands,
Cool like syringa buds,
Firm and silken like pink young peony flowers.

Part Two Creature
第二辑 生灵

蝈蝈和蟋蟀

On the Grasshopper and Cricket

John Keats

The poetry of earth is never dead:
When all the birds are faint with the hot sun,
And hide in cooling trees, a voice will run
From hedge to hedge about the new-mown mead;

That is the Grasshopper's. He takes the lead
In summer luxury; he has never done
With his delights, for when tired out with fun
He rests at ease beneath some pleasant weed.

The poetry of earth is ceasing never:
On a lone winter evening, when the frost
Has wrought a silence, from the stove there shrills
The Cricket's song, in warmth increasing ever,
And seems to one in drowsiness half lost,
The Grasshopper's among some grassy hills.

母牛

The Cow

Robert Louis Stevenson

The friendly cow, all red and white,
I love with all my heart:
She gives me cream with all her might,
To eat with apple tart.

She wanders lowing here and there,
And yet she cannot stray,
All in the pleasant open air,
The pleasant light of day;

And blown by all the winds that pass
And wet with all the showers,
She walks among the meadow grass
And eats the meadow flowers.

苍蝇

The Fly

William Blake

Little Fly,
Thy summer's play
My thoughtless hand
Has brushed away.

Am not I
A fly like thee?
Or art not thou
A man like me?

For I dance
And drink, and sing,
Till some blind hand
Shall brush my wing.

If thought is life
And strength and breath
And the want
Of thought is death;

Then am I
A happy fly,
If I live,
Or if I die.

小羊羔

The Lamb

William Blake

Little Lamb, who made thee?
Dost thou know who made thee?
Gave thee life, and bid thee feed
By the stream and o'er the mead;
Gave thee clothing of delight,
Softest clothing, woolly, bright;
Gave thee such a tender voice,
Making all the vales rejoice?
Little Lamb, who made thee?
Dost thou know who made thee?

Little Lamb, I'll tell thee,
Little Lamb, I'll tell thee:
He is called by thy name,
For he calls himself a Lamb.
He is meek, and he is mild;
He became a little child.
I a child, and thou a lamb.
We are called by his name.
Little Lamb, God bless thee!
Little Lamb, God bless thee!

老虎

The Tiger

William Blake

Tiger, tiger, burning bright
In the forests of the night,
What immortal hand or eye
Could frame thy fearful symmetry?

In what distant deeps or skies
Burnt the fire of thine eyes?
On what wings dare he aspire?
What the hand dare seize the fire?

And what shoulder and what art
Could twist the sinews of thy heart?
And when thy heart began to beat,
What dread hand and what dread feet?

What the hammer? what the chain?
In what furnace was thy brain?
What the anvil? What dread grasp
Dare its deadly terrors clasp?

When the stars threw down their spears,
And water'd heaven with their tears,
Did He smile his work to see?
Did He who made the lamb make thee?

Tiger, tiger, burning bright
In the forests of the night,
What immortal hand or eye
Dare frame thy fearful symmetry?

田鼠

The Fieldmouse

Cecil Frances Alexander

Where the acorn tumbles down,
Where the ash tree sheds its berry,
With your fur so soft and brown,
With your eye so round and merry,
Scarcely moving the long grass,
Fieldmouse, I can see you pass.

Little thing, in what dark den,
Lie you all the winter sleeping?
Till warm weather comes again,
Then once more I see you peeping
Round about the tall tree roots,
Nibbling at their fallen fruits.

Fieldmouse, fieldmouse, do not go,
Where the farmer stacks his treasure,
Find the nut that falls below,
Eat the acorn at your pleasure,

But you must not steal the grain
He has stacked with so much pain.

Make your hole where mosses spring,
Underneath the tall oak's shadow,
Pretty, quiet harmless thing,
Play about the sunny meadow.
Keep away from corn and house,
None will harm you, little mouse.

致蝴蝶

To a Butterfly

William Wordsworth

I've watched you now a full half-hour,
Self-poised upon that yellow flower;
And, little Butterfly! indeed
I know not if you sleep or feed.
How motionless!—not frozen seas
More motionless! and then
What joy awaits you, when the breeze
Hath found you out among the trees,
And calls you forth again!

This plot of orchard-ground is ours;
My trees they are, my Sister's flowers;
Here rest your wing when they are weary;
Here lodge as in a sanctuary!

Come often to us, fear no wrong;
Sit near us on the bough!
We'll talk of sunshine and of song,
And summer days, when we were young;
Sweet childish days, that were as long
As twenty days are now.

鹰

The Eagle

Alfred Lord Tennyson

He clasps the crag with crooked hands;
Close to the sun in lonely lands,
Ring'd with the azure world, he stands.

The wrinkled sea beneath him crawls;
He watches from his mountain walls,
And like a thunderbolt he falls.

猫头鹰

The Owl

Alfred Lord Tennyson

When cats run home and light is come,
And dew is cold upon the ground,
And the far-off stream is dumb,

And the whirring sail goes round,
And the whirring sail goes round;
Alone and warming his five wits,
The white owl in the belfry sits.

When merry milkmaids click the latch,
And rarely smells the new-mown hay,
And the cock hath sung beneath the thatch
Twice or thrice his roundelay,
Twice or thrice his roundelay;
Alone and warming his five wits,
The white owl in the belfry sits.

蜂鸟

Humming-Bird

David Herbert Lawrence

I can imagine, in some otherworld
Primeval-dumb, far back
In that most awful stillness, that only gasped and hummed,
Humming-birds raced down the avenues.

Before anything had a soul,
While life was a heave of Matter, half inanimate,
This little bit chipped off in brilliance
And went whizzing through the slow, vast, succulent stems.

I believe there were no flowers, then
In the world where the humming-bird flashed ahead of creation.
I believe he pierced the slow vegetable veins with his long beak.

Probably he was big
As mosses, and little lizards, they say were once big.
Probably he was a jabbing, terrifying monster.

We look at him through the wrong end of the long telescope of Time,
Luckily for us.

鸭子的小调

Ducks' Ditty

Kenneth Grahame

All along the backwater,
Through the rushes tall,
Ducks are a-dabbling.
Up tails all!

Ducks' tails, drakes' tails,
Yellow feet a-quiver,
Yellow bills all out of sight
Busy in the river!

Slushy green undergrowth
Where the roach swim—
Here we keep our larder,
Cool and full and dim.

Everyone for what he likes!
We like to be
Heads down, tails up,
Dabbling free!

High in the blue above
Swifts whirl and call—
We are down a-dabbling,
Up tails all!

两只小猫

Two Little Kittens

Jane Taylor

Two little kittens
One stormy night,
Begun to quarrel,
And then to fight.

One had a mouse
And the other had none;
And that's the way
The quarrel begun.

"I'll have that mouse,"
Said the bigger cat.
"You'll have that mouse?
We'll see about that!"

"I will have that mouse,"
Said the tortoise-shell;
And, spitting and scratching,
On her sister she fell.

I've told you before
'Twas a stormy night,
When these two kittens
Began to fight.

The old woman took
The sweeping broom,
And swept them both
Right out of the room.

The ground was covered
With frost and snow,
They had lost the mouse,
And had nowhere to go.

So they lay and shivered
Beside the door,
Till the old woman finished
Sweeping the floor.

And then they crept in

As quiet as mice,

All wet with snow

And as cold as ice.

They found it much better

That stormy night,

To lie by the fire,

Than to quarrel and fight.

蜘蛛

The Spider

Jane Taylor

"Oh, look at that great ugly spider!" said Ann;

And screaming, she brush'd it away with her fan;

"'Tis a frightful black creature as ever can be,

I wish that it would not come crawling on me."

"Indeed," said her mother, "I'll venture to say,

The poor thing will try to keep out of your way;

For after the fright, and the fall, and the pain,

It has much more occasion than you to complain.

"But why should you dread the poor insect, my dear?

If it hurt you, there'd be some excuse for your fear;

But its little black legs, as it hurried away,

Did but tickle your arm, as they went, I dare say.

"For them to fear us we must grant to be just,

Who in less than a moment can tread them to dust;

But certainly we have no cause for alarm;

For, were they to try, they could do us no harm.

"Now look! it has got to its home; do you see

What a delicate web it has spun in the tree?

Why here, my dear Ann, is a lesson for you:

Come learn from this spider what patience can do!

"And when at your business you're tempted to play,

Recollect what you see in this insect to-day,

Or else, to your shame, it may seem to be true,

That a poor little spider is wiser than you."

一只小鸟沿小径走来

A Bird Came Down The Walk

Emily Dickinson

A Bird came down the Walk—

He did not know I saw—

He bit an Angle worm in halves

And ate the fellow, raw,

And then he drank a Dew

From a convenient Grass—

And then hopped sidewise to the Wall

To let a Beetle pass—

He glanced with rapid eyes

That hurried all around—
They looked like frightened Beads, I thought—
He stirred his Velvet Head

Like one in danger; Cautious,
I offered him a Crumb
And he unrolled his feathers
And rowed him softer home—

Than Oars divide the Ocean,
Too silver for a seam—
Or Butterflies, off Banks of Noon,
Leap, plashless as they swim.

草丛中一个细长的家伙

A Narrow Fellow In The Grass

Emily Dickinson

A narrow Fellow in the Grass
Occasionally rides;
You may have met Him—did you not
His notice sudden is.

The Grass divides as with a Comb,
A spotted shaft is seen;
And then it closes at your feet
And opens further on.

He likes a Boggy Acre,
A Floor too cool for Corn.
Yet when a Boy, and Barefoot,
I more than once at Noon,
Have passed, I thought, a Whip lash
Unbraiding in the Sun
When stooping to secure it,
It wrinkled, and was gone.

Several of Nature's People
I know, and they know me;
I feel for them a transport
Of cordiality;

But never met this Fellow,
Attended, or alone,
Without a tighter breathing,
And Zero at the Bone.

猫和月亮

The Cat and Moon

William Butler Yeats

The cat went here and there
And the moon spun like a top,
And the nearest kin of the moon,
The creeping cat, looked up.

Black Minnaloushe stared at the moon,

For, wander and wail as he would,

The pure cold light in the sky

Troubled his animal blood.

Minnaloushe runs in the grass

Lifting his delicate feet.

Do you dance, Minnaloushe, do you dance?

When two close kindred meet

What better than call a dance?

Maybe the moon may learn,

Tired of that courtly fashion,

A new dance turn.

Minnaloushe creeps through the grass

From moonlit place to place,

The sacred moon overhead

Has taken a new phrase.

Does Minnaloushe know that his pupils

Will pass from change to change.

And that from round to crescent,

From crescent to round they range?

Minnaloushe creeps through the grass

Alone, important and wise.

And lifts to the changing moon

His changing eyes.

小蜜蜂何其忙碌

How Doth the Little Busy Bee

Isaac Watts

How doth the little busy bee

Improve each shining hour,

And gather honey all the day

From every opening flower!

How skillfully she builds her cell!

How neat she spreads the wax!

And labors hard to store it well

With the sweet food she makes.

In works of labor or of skill,

I would be busy too;

For Satan finds some mischief still

For idle hands to do.

In books, or work, or healthful play,

Let my first years be passed,

That I may give for every day

Some good account at last.

鹰的嬉戏

The Dalliance of the Eagles

Walt Whitman

Skirting the river road, (my forenoon walk, my rest,)

Skyward in air a sudden muffled sound, the dalliance of the eagles,

The rushing amorous contact high in space together,

The clinching interlocking claws, a living, fierce, gyrating wheel,
Four beating wings, two beaks, a swirling mass tight grappling,
In tumbling turning clustering loops, straight downward falling,
Till o'er the river pois'd, the twain yet one, a moment's lull,
A motionless still balance in the air, then parting, talons loosing,
Upward again on slow-firm pinions slanting, their separate diverse flight,
She hers, he his, pursuing.

一只沉默而坚忍的蜘蛛

A Noiseless Patient Spider

Walt Whitman

A noiseless, patient spider,
I mark'd, where, on a little promontory, it stood, isolated;
Mark'd how, to explore the vacant, vast surrounding,
It launch'd forth filament, filament, filament, out of itself;
Ever unreeling them—ever tirelessly speeding them.

And you, O my Soul, where you stand,
Surrounded, surrounded, in measureless oceans of space,
Ceaselessly musing, venturing, throwing, — seeking the spheres, to connect them;
Till the bridge you will need, be form'd—till the ductile anchor hold;
Till the gossamer thread you fling, catch somewhere, O my Soul.

Part Three World
第三辑 世界

希望是带羽毛的东西
Hope Is the Thing with Feathers

Emily Dickinson

Hope is the thing with feathers
That perches in the soul,
And sings the tune without the words,
And never stops at all,

And sweetest in the gale is heard;
And sore must be the storm
That could abash the little bird
That kept so many warm.

I've heard it in the chillest land,
And on the strangest sea;
Yet, never, in extremity,
It asked a crumb of me.

我是无名之辈！你是谁？
I'm Nobody! Who Are You?

Emily Dickinson

I'm nobody! Who are you?
Are you nobody, too?
Then there's a pair of us—don't tell!
They'd banish us, you know.

How dreary to be somebody!
How public, like a frog
To tell your name the livelong day
To an admiring bog!

没有一艘快船能像一本书
There Is No Frigate Like a Book

Emily Dickinson

There is no frigate like a book

185

To take us lands away,
Nor any coursers like a page
Of prancing poetry.

This traverse may the poorest take
Without oppress of toll;
How frugal is the chariot
That bears a human soul!

雪
Snow

Philip Edward Thomas

In the gloom of whiteness,
In the great silence of snow,
A child was sighing
And bitterly saying: "Oh,
They have killed a white bird up there on her nest,
The down is fluttering from her breast!"
And still it fell through that dusky brightness
On the child crying for the bird of the snow.

回答一个孩子的问题
Answer to a Child's Question

Samuel Taylor Coleridge

Do you ask what the birds say? The sparrow, the dove,
The linnet, and thrush say, "I love and I love!"
In the winter they're silent, the wind is so strong;
What it says I don't know, but it sings a loud song.
But green leaves and blossoms, and sunny warm weather,
And singing, and loving, all come back together.
Then the lark is so brimful of gladness and love,
The green fields below him, the blue sky above,
That he sings, and he sings, and forever sings he—
"I love my Love, and my Love loves me!"

致水仙
To Daffodils

Robert Herrick

Fair Daffodils, we weep to see
You haste away so soon;
As yet the early-rising sun
Has not attain'd his noon.
Stay, stay,
Until the hasting day
Has run
But to the even-song;
And, having pray'd together, we
Will go with you along.

We have short time to stay, as you,

We have as short a spring;
As quick a growth to meet decay,
As you, or anything.
We die
As your hours do, and dry
Away,
Like to the summer's rain;
Or as the pearls of morning's dew,
Ne'er to be found again.

秋天的火焰
Autumn Fires

Robert Louis Stevenson

In the other gardens
And all up the vale,
From the autumn bonfires
See the smoke trail!

Pleasant summer over
And all the summer flowers,
The red fire blazes,
The grey smoke towers.

Sing a song of seasons!
Something bright in all!
Flowers in the summer,
Fires in the fall!

大风夜
Windy Nights

Robert Louis Stevenson

Whenever the moon and stars are set,
Whenever the wind is high,
All night long in the dark and wet,
A man goes riding by.
Late in the night when the fires are out,
Why does he gallop and gallop about?

Whenever the trees are crying aloud,
And ships are tossed at sea,
By, on the highway, low and loud,
By, at the gallop goes he.
But at the gallop he goes, and then
By he comes back at the gallop again.

燧石
Flint

Christina Georgina Rossetti

An emerald is as green as grass,
A ruby red as blood;
A sapphire shines as blue heaven;
A flint lies in the mud.

A diamond is a brilliant stone,
To catch the world's desire;
An opal holds a fiery spark;
But a flint holds fire.

顿悟

Sudden Light

Dante Gabriel Rossetti

I have been here before,
But when or how I cannot tell:
I know the grass beyond the door,
The sweet keen smell,
The sighing sound, the lights around the shore.

You have been mine before—
How long ago I may not know:
But just when at that swallow's soar
Your neck turn'd so,
Some veil did fall—I knew it all of yore.

Has this been thus before?
And shall not thus time's eddying flight
Still with our lives our love restore
In death's despite,
And day and night yield one delight once more?

我

Me

Walter de la Mare

As long as I live
I shall always be
My Self—and no other,
Just me.

Like a tree—
Willow, elder,
Aspen, thorn,
Or cypress forlorn.

Like a flower,
For its hour—

Primrose, or pink,
Or a violet—
Sunned by the sun
And with dewdrops wet.

Always just me.
Till the day come on
When I leave this body,
It's all then done,
And the spirit within it
Is gone.

诗人的歌

The Poet's Song

Alfred Lord Tennyson

The rain had fallen, the Poet arose,
He pass'd by the town and out of the street;
A light wind blew from the gates of the sun,
And waves of shadow went over the wheat;
And he sat him down in a lonely place,
And chanted a melody loud and sweet,
That made the wild-swan pause in her cloud,
And the lark drop down at his feet.
The swallow stopt as he hunted the fly,
The snake slipt under a spray,
The wild hawk stood with the down on his beak,
And stared, with his foot on the prey;
And the nightingale thought, "I have sung many songs,
But never a one so gay,
For he sings of what the world will be
When the years have died away."

万物明亮又美丽

All things bright and beautiful

Cecil Frances Alexander

All things bright and beautiful,
All creatures great and small,
All things wise and wonderful:
The Lord God made them all.

Each little flower that opens,
Each little bird that sings,
He made their glowing colors,
He made their tiny wings.

The purple-headed mountains,
The river running by,
The sunset and the morning
That brightens up the sky.

The cold wind in the winter,
The pleasant summer sun,
The ripe fruits in the garden,
He made them every one.

He gave us eyes to see them,
And lips that we might tell
How great is God Almighty,
Who has made all things well.

咒语

Spellbound

Emily Bronte

The night is darkening round me,

The wild winds coldly blow;
But a tyrant spell has bound me
And I cannot, cannot go.

The giant trees are bending
Their bare boughs weighed with snow.
And the storm is fast descending,
And yet I cannot go.

Clouds beyond clouds above me,
Wastes beyond wastes below;
But nothing drear can move me;
I will not, cannot go.

黄金国度

Eldorado

Edgar Allan Poe

Gaily bedight,
A gallant knight,
In sunshine and in shadow,
Had journeyed long,
Singing a song,
In search of Eldorado.

But he grew old—
This knight so bold—
And o'er his heart a shadow

Fell as he found
No spot of ground
That looked like Eldorado.

And, as his strength
Failed him at length,
He met a pilgrim shadow—
"Shadow," said he,
"Where can it be—
This land of Eldorado?"

"Over the Mountains
Of the Moon,
Down the Valley of the Shadow,
Ride, boldly ride,"
The shade replied—
"If you seek for Eldorado!"

人的四季

The Human Seasons

John Keats

Four Seasons fill the measure of the year;
There are four seasons in the mind of man:
He has his lusty Spring, when fancy clear
Takes in all beauty with an easy span:

He has his Summer, when luxuriously

Spring's honied cud of youthful thought he loves
To ruminate, and by such dreaming high
Is nearest unto heaven: quiet coves

His soul has in its Autumn, when his wings
He furleth close; contented so to look
On mists in idleness—to let fair things
Pass by unheeded as a threshold brook.

He has his Winter too of pale misfeature,
Or else he would forego his mortal nature.

花园围墙那边
Over the Garden Wall

Eleanor Farjeon

Over the garden wall
Where unseen children play,
Somebody threw a ball
One fine summer day.
I caught it as it came
Straight from the hand unknown,
Playing a happy game
It would not play alone.

A pretty ball with bands
Of gold and stars of blue;
I turned it in my hands

And wondered, then I threw
Over the garden wall
Again the treasure round—
And somebody caught the ball
With a laughing sound.

那是在很久以前
It Was Long Ago

Eleanor Farjeon

I'll tell you, shall I, something I remember?
Something that still means a great deal to me.
It was long ago.

A dusty road in summer I remember,
A mountain, and an old house, and a tree
That stood, you know,

Behind the house. An old woman I remember
In a red shawl with a grey cat on her knee
Humming under a tree.

She seemed the oldest thing I can remember.
But then perhaps I was not more than three.
It was long ago.

I dragged on the dusty road, and I remember
How the old woman looked over the fence at me

And seemed to know

How it felt to be three, and called out, I remember
"Do you like bilberries and cream for tea?"
I went under the tree.

And while she hummed, and the cat purred, I remember
How she filled a saucer with berries and cream for me
So long ago.

Such berries and such cream as I remember
I never had seen before, and never see
Today, you know.

And that is almost all I can remember,
The house, the mountain, the gray cat on her knee,
Her red shawl, and the tree,

And the taste of the berries, the feel of the sun I remember,
And the smell of everything that used to be
So long ago,

Till the heat on the road outside again I remember
And how the long dusty road seemed to have for me
No end, you know.

That is the farthest thing I can remember.
It won't mean much to you. It does to me.
Then I grew up, you see.

打哈欠
Yawning

Eleanor Farjeon

Sometimes—I'm sorry—but sometimies,
Sometimes, yes, sometimes I'm bored.
It may be because I'm an idiot;
It may be because I'm floored;

It may be because it is raining,
It may be because it is hot,
It may be because I have eaten
Too much, or because I have not.

But sometimes I cannot help yawning
(I'm sorry!) the whole morning through—
And when Teacher's turning her back on us,
It may be that she's yawing too.

在下午的山岗上
Afternoon on a Hill

Edna St. Vincent Millay

I will be the gladdest thing
Under the sun!
I will touch a hundred flowers

And not pick one.

I will look at cliffs and clouds
With quiet eyes,
Watch the wind bow down the grass,
And the grass rise.

And when lights begin to show
Up from the town,
I will mark which must be mine,
And then start down!

未来

The Future

Charles Cros

Black poppies and the fading cornflowers
In the ripe hay by the stable,
Yellowed letters of my respectable grandfather,
Full of old fashioned vows to my grandmother,

Snuff box of my great uncle,
Backgammon board inlaid on the little table,
Carry me away, so I can imagine a time
When my verses will carry you away, you who are
not yet born.

For I was very much alive. Every wind which blew
brought
The odor of hawthorn blossoms and lilacs.
The sound of kisses drowned out the tolling of bells.

O readers to come, who will live in the joy
Of sixteen, of lilacs and first kisses,
Your loves will rejoice my rotting bones.

Part Four Nature and Others
第四辑 自然及其他

秋颂

Ode to Autumn

John keats

Season of mists and mellow fruitfulness!
Close bosom-friend of the maturing sun;
Conspiring with him how to load and bless
With fruit the vines that round the thatch-eaves run;
To bend with apples the mossed cottage-trees,
And fill all fruit with ripeness to the core;
To swell the gourd, and plump the hazel shells
With a sweet kernel; to set budding more,
And still more, later flowers for the bees,
Until they think warm days will never cease,
For Summer has o'erbrimmed their clammy cells.

Who hath not seen thee oft amid thy store?
Sometimes whoever seeks abroad may find
Thee sitting careless on a granary floor,
Thy hair soft-lifted by the winnowing wind;
Or on a half-reaped furrow sound asleep,
Drowsed with the fume of poppies, while thy hook
Spares the next swath and all its twined flowers;
And sometimes like a gleaner thou dost keep
Steady thy laden head across a brook;
Or by a cider-press, with patient look,
Thou watchest the last oozings, hours by hours.

Where are the songs of Spring? Ay, where are they?
Think not of them, thou hast thy music too,
While barred clouds bloom the soft-dying day
And touch the stubble-plains with rosy hue;
Then in a wailful choir the small gnats mourn
Among the river sallows, borne aloft
Or sinking as the light wind lives or dies;
And full-grown lambs loud bleat from hilly bourn;
Hedge-crickets sing, and now with treble soft
The redbreast whistles from a garden-croft;
And gathering swallows twitter in the skies.

多少诗人给时间的流逝镀上了金

How Many Bards Gild the Lapses of Time

John Keats

How many bards gild the lapses of time!
A few of them have ever been the food
Of my delighted fancy—I could brood
Over their beauties, earthly, or sublime:
And often, when I sit me down to rhyme,
These will in throngs before my mind intrude:
But no confusion, no disturbance rude
Do they occasion; 'tis a pleasing chime.
So the unnumbered sounds that evening store;
The songs of birds the whispering of the leaves
The voice of waters—the great bell that heaves
With solemn sound, —and thousand others more,
That distance of recognizance bereaves,
Makes pleasing music, and not wild uproar.

啊，孤独！如果我必须与你同住

O Solitude! If I Must With Thee Dwell

John Keats

O Solitude! if I must with thee dwell,
Let it not be among the jumbled heap
Of murky buildings: climb with me the steep,
Nature's observatory—whence the dell,
In flowery slopes, its river's crystal swell,
May seem a span; let me thy vigils keep
'Mongst boughs pavilioned, where the deer's swift leap
Startles the wild bee from the foxglove bell.
But though I'll gladly trace these scenes with thee,
Yet the sweet converse of an innocent mind,
Whose words are images of thoughts refined,
Is my soul's pleasure; and it sure must be
Almost the highest bliss of human-kind,
When to thy haunts two kindred spirits flee.

黄水仙

The Daffodils

William Wordsworth

I wandered lonely as a cloud
That floats on high o'er vales and hills,
When all at once I saw a crowd,
A host, of golden daffodils;
Beside the lake, beneath the trees,
Fluttering and dancing in the breeze.

Continuous as the stars that shine
And twinkle on the milky way,

They stretched in never-ending line
Along the margin of a bay:
Ten thousand saw I at a glance,
Tossing their heads in sprightly dance.

The waves beside them danced; but they
Out-did the sparkling waves in glee:
A poet could not but be gay,
In such a jocund company:
I gazed—and gazed—but little thought
What wealth the show to me had brought:

For oft, when on my couch I lie
In vacant or in pensive mood,
They flash upon that inward eye
Which is the bliss of solitude;
And then my heart with pleasure fills,
And dances with the daffodils.

啊，向日葵
Ah! Sun-flower

William Blake

Ah Sun-flower! Weary of time,
Who countest the steps of the Sun;
Seeking after that sweet golden clime
Where the travellers journey is done.

Where the Youth pined away with desire,
And the pale Virgin shrouded in snow;
Arise from their graves and aspire,
Where my Sun-flower wishes to go.

一片残雪
A Patch of Old Snow

Robert Frost

There's a patch of old snow in a corner
That I should have guessed
Was a blow-away paper the rain
Had brought to rest.

It is speckled with grime as if
Small print overspread it,
The news of a day I've forgotten—
If I ever read it.

未走的路
The Road Not Taken

Robert Frost

Two roads diverged in a yellow wood,
And sorry I could not travel both

And be one traveler, long I stood
And looked down one as far as I could
To where it bent in the undergrowth;

Then took the other, as just as fair,
And having perhaps the better claim,
Because it was grassy and wanted wear;
Though as for that the passing there
Had worn them really about the same,

And both that morning equally lay
In leaves no step had trodden black.
Oh, I kept the first for another day!
Yet knowing how way leads on to way,
I doubted if I should ever come back.

I shall be telling this with a sigh
Somewhere ages and ages hence:
Two roads diverged in a wood, and I—
I took the one less traveled by,
And that has made all the difference.

雪夜林边驻足

Stopping by Woods on a Snowy Evening

Robert Frost

Whose woods these are I think I know.
His house is in the village, though;
He will not see me stopping here
To watch his woods fill up with snow.

My little horse must think it queer
To stop without a farmhouse near
Between the woods and frozen lake
The darkest evening of the year.

He gives his harness bells a shake
To ask if there is some mistake.
The only other sound's the sweep
Of easy wind and downy flake.

The woods are lovely, dark and deep,
But I have promises to keep,
And miles to go before I sleep,
And miles to go before I sleep.

茵尼斯弗利湖岛

The Lake Isle of Innisfree

William Butler Yeats

I will arise and go now, and go to Innisfree,
And a small cabin build there, of clay and wattles made:
Nine bean-rows will I have there, a hive for the honey-bee,

And live alone in the bee-loud glade.

And I shall have some peace there, for peace comes dropping slow,
Dropping from the veils of the morning to where the cricket sings;
There midnight's all a glimmer, and noon a purple glow,
And evening full of the linnet's wings.

I will arise and go now, for always night and day
I hear lake water lapping with low sounds by the shore;
While I stand on the roadway, or on the pavements grey,
I hear it in the deep heart's core.

美德

Virtue

George Herbert

Sweet day, so cool, so calm, so bright,
The bridal of the earth and sky;
The dew shall weep thy fall to-night,
For thou must die.

Sweet rose, whose hue angry and brave
Bids the rash gazer wipe his eye;
Thy root is ever in its grave,
And thou must die.

Sweet spring, full of sweet days and roses,
A box where sweets compacted lie;
My music shows ye have your closes,
And all must die.

Only a sweet and virtuous soul,
Like season'd timber, never gives;
But though the whole world turn to coal,
Then chiefly lives.

本能

Instinct

Edith Irene Södergran

My body is a mystery.
As long as this brittle thing is alive
You will feel its power.
I will save the world.
That is why Eros' blood is coursing through my lips
And Eros' gold runs through my tired curls.
I need only to look,
Weary or in pain: the earth is mine.
When I lie exhausted on my bed
I know: in this weakened hand lies the fate of the earth.

It is power that trembles in my shoe,

It is power that moves in the folds of my dress,

And it is power, fearing no abyss, that stands before you.

我童年的树木
My Childhood Trees

Edith Irene Södergran

My childhood trees stand tall in the grass

And shake their heads: what has become of you?

Rows of pillars stand like reproaches: you are unworthy

To walk beneath us!

You are a child and should know everything,

So why are you fettered by your illness?

You have become a human, alien and hateful.

As a child, you talked with us for hours,

Your eyes were wise.

No we would like to tell you the secrets of your life:

The key to all the secrets lies in the grass by the raspberry patch.

We want to shake you up, you sleeper,

We want to wake you, dead one, from your sleep.

林中湖泊
Forest Lake

Edith Irene Södergran

I was alone on a sunny shore

By the forest's pale blue lake,

In the sky floated a single cloud

And on the water a single isle.

The ripe sweetness of summer dripped

In beads from every tree

And straight into my opened heart

A tiny drop ran down.

星
Star

Edith Irene Södergran

When darkness fell

I stood on the steps to listen to;

Stars swarm in the garden

I stood in the dark.

Listen to the sound of landing a star!

You do not walk barefoot in the grass,

My garden is full of star fragments.

我看见路易斯安那有一棵橡树在生长

I Saw in Louisiana a live-Oak Growing

Walt Whitman

I saw in Louisiana a live-oak growing,
All alone stood it and the moss hung down from the branches,
Without any companion it grew there uttering joyous leaves of dark green,
And its look, rude, unbending, lusty, made me think of myself,
But I wondered how it could utter joyous leaves standing alone there without its friend near, for I knew I could not,
And I broke off a twig with a certain number of leaves upon it, and twined around it a little moss,
And brought it away, and I have placed it in sight in my room,
It is not needed to remind me as of my own dear friends,
(For I believe lately I think of little else than of them,)
Yet it remains to me a curious token, it makes me think of manly love;
For all that, and though the live-oak glistens there in Louisiana
solitary in a wide flat space,
Uttering joyous leaves all its life without a friend or lover near,
I know very well I could not.

当我听到那博学的天文学家

When I Heard the Learn'd Astronomer

Walt Whitman

When I heard the learn'd astronomer;
When the proofs, the figures, were ranged in columns before me;
When I was shown the charts and the diagrams, to add, divide, and measure them;
When I, sitting, heard the astronomer, where he lectured with much applause in the lecture-room,
How soon, unaccountable, I became tired and sick;
Till rising and gliding out, I wander'd off by myself,
In the mystical moist night-air, and from time to time,
Look'd up in perfect silence at the stars.

奇迹

Miracles

Walt Whitman

Why, who makes much of a miracle?
As to me I know of nothing else but miracles,
Whether I walk the streets of Manhattan,
Or dart my sight over the roofs of houses toward the

sky,
Or wade with naked feet along the beach just in the edge of the water,
Or stand under trees in the woods,
Or talk by day with any one I love, or sleep in the bed at night with any one I love,
Or sit at table at dinner with the rest,
Or look at strangers opposite me riding in the car,
Or watch honey-bees busy around the hive of a summer forenoon,
Or animals feeding in the fields,
Or birds, or the wonderfulness of insects in the air,
Or the wonderfulness of the sundown, or of stars shining so quiet and bright,
Or the exquisite delicate thin curve of the new moon in spring;
These with the rest, one and all, are to me miracles,
The whole referring, yet each distinct and in its place.

To me every hour of the light and dark is a miracle,
Every cubic inch of space is a miracle,
Every square yard of the surface of the earth is spread with the same,
Every foot of the interior swarms with the same.
To me the sea is a continual miracle,
The fishes that swim—the rocks—the motion of the waves—the ships with men in them,
What stranger miracles are there?

记忆

Memory

Thomas Bailey Aldrich

My mind lets go a thousand things
Like dates of wars and deaths of kings,
And yet recalls the very hour—
'Twas noon by yonder village tower,
And on the last blue noon in May—
The wind came briskly up this way,
Crisping the brook beside the road;
Then, pausing here, set down its load
Of pine-scents, and shook listlessly
Two petals from that wild-rose tree.

致水鸟

To a Waterfowl

William Cullen Bryant

Whither, midst falling dew,
While glow the heavens with the last steps of day,
Far, through their rosy depths, dost thou pursue
Thy solitary way?

Vainly the fowler's eye

Might mark thy distant flight to do thee wrong,
As, darkly seen against the crimson sky,
Thy figure floats along.

Seek'st thou the plashy brink
Of weedy lake, or marge of river wide,
Or where the rocking billows rise and sink
On the chafed ocean-side?

There is a Power whose care
Teaches thy way along that pathless coast—
The desert and illimitable air—
Lone wandering, but not lost.

All day thy wings have fanned,
At that far height, the cold, thin atmosphere,
Yet stoop not, weary, to the welcome land,
Though the dark night is near.

And soon that toil shall end;
Soon shalt thou find a summer home, and rest,
And scream among thy fellows; reeds shall bend,
Soon, o'er thy sheltered nest.

Thou'rt gone, the abyss of heaven
Hath swallowed up thy form; yet, on my heart
Deeply hath sunk the lesson thou hast given,
And shall not soon depart.

He who, from zone to zone,
Guides through the boundless sky thy certain flight,
In the long way that I must tread alone,
Will lead my steps aright.

缪斯

Muse

Anna Andreyevna Akhmatova

When, in the night, I wait for her,
impatient, Life seems to me, as hanging by a thread.
What just means liberty, or youth, or approbation,
When compared with the gentle piper's tread?

And she came in, threw out the mantle's edges,
Declined to me with a sincere heed. I say to her,
"Did you dictate the Pages Of Hell to Dante?"
She answers, "Yes, I did."

我不与人争

I Strove With None

Walter Savage Landor

I strove with none, for none was worth my strife.
Nature I loved and, next to Nature, Art;
I warm'd both hands before the fire of life;
It sinks, and I am ready to depart.

作者介绍

萨拉·柯勒律治（Sara Coleridge，1802—1852年），英国翻译家、童诗作家，以编辑其父塞缪尔·泰勒·柯勒律治的作品而闻名。

列维斯·卡洛尔（Lewis Carroll，1832—1898年），英国著名的数学家。卡洛尔是他发表《爱丽丝漫游奇境记》时首次使用的笔名。他多才多艺，兴趣广泛，在小说、童话、诗歌、逻辑等方面都有很深的造诣。自1854年出版两部诗集之后，他一直在各种杂志上发表文学作品。1865年，以《爱丽丝漫游奇境记》的发表而轰动文坛，1871年他又出版了《爱丽丝镜中奇遇记》，这两部童话风靡世界，成为儿童文学经典。

詹姆斯·霍格（James Hogg，1770—1835年），苏格兰诗人、小说家，同时用苏格兰语和英语写作，青年时以牧羊和农作为生，通过阅读自学成才。

埃德加·爱伦·坡（Edgar Allan Poe，1809—1849年），19世纪美国诗人、小说家和文学评论家，美国浪漫主义思潮时期的重要成员。

爱德华·利尔（Edward Lear，1812—1888年），英国画家、插画家、音乐家、作家和诗人，他为儿童写作谐趣诗并绘制插图，其中包括《猫头鹰和小猫咪》等，使五行打油诗作为一种幽默诗歌形式而得到推广。

珀西·比希·雪莱（Percy Bysshe Shelley，1792—1822年），英国著名作家、浪漫主义诗人，被认为是历史上最出色的英语诗人之一。

阿尔弗雷德·丁尼生（Alfred Lord Tennyson，1809—1892 年），英国维多利亚时代最受欢迎及最具特色的诗人，代表作品有组诗《悼念》。

约翰·济慈（John Keats，1795—1821 年），杰出的英国诗人作家之一，与雪莱、拜伦齐名，被推崇为欧洲浪漫主义运动的杰出代表。

克里斯蒂娜·吉奥尔吉娜·罗塞蒂（Christina Georgina Rossetti，1830—1894 年），19 世纪英国文坛上杰出的女诗人之一。

茱莉亚·阿比盖尔·弗莱彻·卡妮（Julia Abigail Fletcher Carney，1823—1908 年），19 世纪美国教育家和诗人，她的很多作品都被谱成曲，入选美国学校教科书或教会圣歌。

威廉·布莱克（William Blake，1757—1827 年），英国第一位重要的浪漫主义诗人，英国文学史上最重要的伟大诗人之一。主要诗作有诗集《天真之歌》《经验之歌》等。

塞西尔·弗朗西斯·亚历山大（Cecil Frances Alexander，1818—1895 年），19 世纪英国备受欢迎的赞美诗作者和抒情诗人，特别是为儿童写作的赞美诗流传甚广。

罗伯特·路易斯·斯蒂文森（Robert Louis Stevenson，1850—1894 年），英国著名的小说家、诗人，新浪漫主义奠基人与杰出代表。他自幼多病，却有惊人的创作力。在他短促的一生中，写下了大量小说、散文、游记、诗歌。代表作有《金银岛》《化身博士》《一个孩子的诗园》等。

威廉·华兹华斯（William Wordsworth，1770—1850年），英国浪漫主义诗人，曾当上桂冠诗人。其诗歌理论动摇了英国古典主义诗学的统治，有力地推动了英国诗歌的革新和浪漫主义运动的发展，系文艺复兴运动以来最重要的英语诗人之一。

艾米莉·勃朗特（Emily Bronte，1818—1848年），19世纪英国作家、诗人，著名的勃朗特三姐妹之一。世界文学名著《呼啸山庄》的作者，这部作品是她一生唯一的一部小说，奠定了她在英国文学史以及世界文学史上的地位。

戴维·赫伯特·劳伦斯（David Herbert Lawrence，1885—1930年），20世纪英国小说家、批评家、诗人、画家。代表作品有《儿子与情人》《虹》《恋爱中的女人》《查泰莱夫人的情人》等。

肯尼斯·格雷厄姆（Kenneth Grahame，1859—1932年），英国童话作家，生于苏格兰爱丁堡，代表作有《柳林风声》《黄金时代》《梦里春秋》等。

珍·泰勒（Jane Taylor，1783—1824年），英国诗人、小说家，《小星星》的原作者。她经常与妹妹安·泰勒合作，姐妹俩都是成名很早的儿童诗作家，合著作有诗集《婴儿启蒙诗》《为幼儿园所作的韵诗》《捉小鸟的石灰树枝》等。珍·泰勒独立创作有儿童小说《年轻人的故事》等。她的创作影响过诗人罗伯特·勃朗宁，就英国文学而言，她揭示内心生活的能力在狄更斯出现之前无人能及。

艾米莉·狄金森（Emily Dickinson，1830—1886年），美国传奇诗人。出生于律师家庭。25岁起弃绝社交，闭门不出，在孤独中埋头写诗30年，留下诗稿1700余首。生前只发表过7首，其余都是在她死后发表。她的诗用平凡亲切的语言描写了爱情、死亡和自然。她的精美技巧使她的诗歌、信件与生活都成了艺术。她被视为20世纪现代主义诗歌的先驱之一，和美国文学之父欧文、诗人惠特曼比肩。

威廉·巴特勒·叶芝（William Butler Yeats，1865—1939年），爱尔兰诗人、剧作家和散文家，20世纪西方最有成就的诗人之一，1923年诺贝尔文学奖得主。

艾萨克·瓦茨（Isaac Watts，1674—1748年），英国17世纪一位多产的圣诗作者，一生创作了大约750首圣诗，被称为"英国圣诗之父"。

沃尔特·惠特曼（Walt Whitman，1819—1892年），美国现代诗和现代文学之父、人文主义者，创造了诗歌的自由体，其代表作品是诗集《草叶集》。

菲利普·爱德华·托马斯（Philip Edward Thomas，1878—1917年），英国诗人、散文家。曾在牛津大学林肯学院学习历史，后在一战中阵亡，被认为是一战时期最重要的诗人之一。

塞缪尔·泰勒·柯勒律治（Samuel Taylor Coleridge，1772—1834年），英国著名诗人、文学评论家，英国浪漫主义文学奠基人之一，一生作诗不辍，中年弃诗从哲。他与华兹华斯的微妙关系，使他成为西方文学史上最令人瞩目的作家之一。

罗伯特·赫里克（Robert Herrick，1591—1674年），英国资产阶级时期和复辟时期所谓"骑士派"诗人之一。他的许多田园抒情诗和爱情诗成为英国诗歌中的名作而永久流传，传世的约1400首诗分别收录在《雅歌》和《西方乐土》中。

但丁·加百利·罗塞蒂（Dante Gabriel Rossetti，1828—1882年），出生于英国维多利亚时期意大利裔的罗塞蒂家族，19世纪英国拉斐尔前派重要代表画家，也是绘画史上少有的取得独特成就的画家兼诗人，作品注重装饰主义。

沃尔特·德·拉·梅尔（Walter de la Mare，1873—1956年），英国诗人，小说家，还发表了大量儿童阅读的诗歌、小说和散文。

依里诺尔·法吉恩（Eleanor Farjeon，1881—1965年），英国儿童文学作家、诗人和剧作家，她的儿童诗和童话作品让她享有盛名，一生为孩子写了几十部作品，为了纪念她，CBC（儿童图书委员会）童书协会还成立了法吉恩儿童文学奖。

埃德娜·圣·文森特·米莱（Edna St. Vincent Millay，1892—1950年），美国诗人兼剧作家，才气逼人。米莱年少家贫，后因诗歌在全国比赛中获奖，才得到资助进入大学就读。1917年，她来到纽约，开始了长盛不衰又饱受争议的作家生涯。1923年，她因《竖琴织工及其他诗篇》获普利策诗歌奖，成为美国史上首位获此殊荣的女性。

夏尔·克罗（Charles Cros，1842—1888年），法国诗人、幽默作家和发明家。他研究出众多改进摄影的方法，包括早期彩色照片处理。

罗伯特·弗罗斯特（Robert Frost，1874—1963年），20世纪最受欢迎的美国诗人之一。他的诗歌多从农村生活中汲取题材，曾获得4次普利策奖。代表作品有《一棵作证的树》《山间》《新罕布什尔》《西去的溪流》《又一片牧场》《林间空地》等。

乔治·赫伯特（George Herbert，1593—1633年），英国诗人、演说家、玄学派圣人，出身于富有的艺术之家，接受过良好的教育，在剑桥大学和议会都曾担任高级职务。他的作品将丰富的感情和清晰的逻辑融为一体，描写生动形象，隐喻出神入化。

伊迪特·伊蕾内·索德格朗（Edith Irene Södergran，1892—1923年），芬兰著名的瑞典语女诗人，北欧文学史上最早的现代主义作家之一。她深受法国象征主义、德国表现主义、俄国未来主义的影响。她一生只出版了四部诗集。伊迪特·伊蕾内·索德格朗被认为是北欧文学史上最伟大的作家之一。直到现在，她仍然影响着许多诗人，尤其是瑞典语的歌词作者。

托马斯·贝利·奥尔德里奇（Thomas Bailey Aldrich，1836—1907年），美国作家、诗人。著有诗集《钟的谣曲》《花与刺》《温德姆塔》。

威廉·卡伦·布莱恩特（William Cullen Bryant，1794—1878年），美国诗人和新闻记者。美国最早期的自然主义诗人之一。作为美国首位重要的自然派诗人，他经常被称为"美国的华兹华斯"。他诗歌中描写的自然风物和谐而柔美，静谧而有节制，使他成为美国的第一位浪漫主义诗人。

安娜·安德烈耶夫娜·阿赫玛托娃（Anna Andreyevna Akhmatova，1889—1966年），俄罗斯文学史上最伟大的女诗人之一，20世纪世界诗歌史上少数堪称"大师级诗人"中的一个，与普希金并称为俄罗斯诗歌的"太阳和月亮"，几代读者把她的诗和诗性人格看作高贵之美的象征。1912年出版第一本诗集《黄昏》后，又相继出版《念珠》《白色云朵》《车前草》《耶稣纪元》及长诗《没有主人公的叙事诗》、组诗《安魂曲》等。

沃尔特·萨维奇·兰多（Walter Savage Landor，1775—1864年），英国诗人和散文家，曾在牛津大学求学。其诗宁静、谨严、隽永，尤其是他的短篇抒情诗和格言诗受人称道。

后　记

　　作为成年人，无论在社会上取得过多么大的成就，获得过怎样的荣誉和声名，也都没有什么值得夸耀的，唯一值得一说的是：所有的成年人都曾经是个孩子。童年的世界充满了神奇，万物生机勃发，似乎所有的事物都是那么有意义，每一个大人都有趣得可笑，每一场雨都会让你的纸船航行得更快，天很高，午后的阳光似乎久久都不移动。童年的记忆是永恒的，我们在内心深处始终还是那个好奇的孩子，最大的梦想也是重新做回那个纯真又智慧的孩子。就像华兹华斯所言："儿童是成人的父亲。"成人要向儿童学习未来。

　　等到我们长大了，似乎就忘记了自己曾经是个孩子，我们用重重文化的外衣将真实的自己严密地包裹起来，慢慢习惯了一场雨只是雨、树只是树、人也只是人的世界。我们忘记了我们曾经置身于一个任何事物本身就有价值的世界，于是开始用计算、用功利、用利害关系看待事物和他人。我们内心中的那个孩子不再说话了，生活也变得索然无味了，而曾经，生活就是乐园，就是爱和永恒。

　　诗歌可以改变我们的生活，诗歌能够带给我们众多妙不可言的看待世界的方式，诗歌就是唤醒我们内心深处那个孩子的最好的工具。守护宝贵的天真，持存敏锐的感性，保持对事物的好奇心，这一直是人类进步的巨大动力，是恢复我们与万物契合、互相成全的亲密关联，诗歌的功用是怎么也说不尽的。遗忘了诗歌，我们的本性会渐渐蒙上了尘土，我们也终将成为童年时最不希望成为的那种无趣的、精神萎靡的、没有灵性的成年人。

作为一位诗人和译者,我从内心深处那个始终醒着的孩子的眼光出发,以成熟诗人的技巧和洞察力,为其他的孩子写一本诗集的愿望由来已久,而翻译也不啻为一种创作,它比之于个人的原创也许还有某种优越性,因为通过翻译,会有更加丰富多彩的他者声音传递过来,于是我选择了用翻译来"创作"。这本书前后花费了我近三年的时间,是在近千首诗歌的阅读中披沙沥金之所得。所选作者有的是致力于儿童诗创作的名家,有的以"成人"诗名世。我发现,很多著名的诗人都给孩子写过诗,或者他们写过的一些普通诗歌碰巧适合孩子阅读,我都从中选取了。

这些诗歌久经时间的考验,具有经典性和权威性,在世界上广为流传,激励和安慰了数代小读者,当然,它们对于成年人也有很大的意义,可以说,这本书也适合成人带着自己的孩子一起阅读。

最后,我想说的是,编译这样一本诗集最初的动因是为我当时尚未出世的孙儿(或孙女)准备的一件"谦卑的礼物"。现在,孙儿玉堂已经5岁多了,我希望这本书能陪伴他成长,我也相信这本书会在他人生的各个阶段给予他勇气。为了达到这个目标,我在翻译时格外用心,译文也反复修订,反复出声朗读,然后再行修订,这定会惠及所有打开这本书的孩子和成人。一想到不知会是哪双手打开它,好奇地窥望书中的世界,并获得快乐和鼓舞,我就感到十分的激动和幸福。

在这里,我也要郑重感谢所有参与本书朗读的声音艺术家,你们美妙的声音将陪伴着也许我们永不能谋面和相识的小读者及大读者们,走过充满美善与冒险的人生。

2020年1月6日于南京孝陵卫罗汉巷